Matched Hearts

Enjoy the read!

Matched Hearts

Cathe Swanson

CATHE SWANSON

The Glory Quilts Series
Book 2

www.catheswanson.com

ISBN-978-1-949412-13-0

Cover art by 85mm Photography, Minneapolis, MN

This is a work of fiction. Names, characters, businesses, places, events, locales, and incidents are either the products of the author's imagination or used in a fictitious manner. Except for Sarah, who is inspired by my favorite grand-niece, Angel Pearson, any resemblance to actual persons, living or dead, or actual events is purely coincidental.

Scripture quotations are from the ESV® Bible (The Holy Bible, English Standard Version®), copyright © 2001 by Crossway, a publishing ministry of Good News Publishers. Used by permission. All rights reserved.

DEDICATION

This book is for my niece, Mellissa Pearson, who is an encouragement and blessing to me. She's a great mother and a fine woman of God.

1

Eleanor Neilson looked around the table at the beloved, beautiful, perfect people and wondered if she was adopted. Her parents, like reigning monarchs, smiled benevolently at their well-behaved family. Even the twins, newly promoted from high chairs, sat upright in their boosters, neatly eating moderate portions of turkey and stuffing. A perfect family of blond, blue-eyed, Minnesotan Swedes.

She hadn't come prepared to dress up for dinner, and when Soren came downstairs sporting a striped shirt and bow tie, she laughed at him. Then Zack and Laurie arrived, bearing pumpkin pies, flowers, and grandchildren. Zack's suit looked like it was made for him. Laurie wore a long corduroy skirt and ivory cashmere sweater, loosely belted around her slim middle. Her floral scarf draped gracefully into elegant folds. If Eleanor wore that, it would collect crumbs like a bib, like a chipmunk, saving morsels to consume later. It might, however, protect her sweater from gravy stains.

"There are bound to be openings for the spring semester, not just at Westerfield but other schools in the area, too. Or you could do substitute work for a while. Eleanor!" Kathy Nielson didn't raise her voice; she just changed the pitch. "I was talking to you."

"Sorry, Mom. I did hear you. I'm going to stick it out up north for a while, though." Lather, rinse, repeat. She'd given up on explanations and discussion. Just say no and take advantage of her mother's refusal to engage in a quarrel at Thanksgiving dinner.

"You may change your mind in January, though," Soren said. "Winter up there is different from being in the city. You could get snowed in at that cabin and no one would find you for weeks."

"And that would be bad because...?"

Her brother ignored the comment and continued. "Uncle Gary will want the cabin, too, like this weekend, for hunting and fishing. You can't leave town every time he wants to have a party."

"You won't want to stay there while the cabin is full of his friends," her mother said. "And he won't want you there."

"I'll stay at his house in town, or I could probably stay with Uncle Carl and Aunt Constance. They've got a lot of room there now. Only Jeffrey, Adrienne and Sarah are still at home. Aunt Violet and Penny are moving out to the farmhouse." Eleanor rather liked the idea of a nomadic existence, but that sentiment would undermine her position. "I'll be looking for a place of my own in the spring."

"You'll be back here by then." Zack handed a napkin to his daughter. "You'd miss Tara and Tyler too much to stay away that long."

"I don't imagine they'll change much by Christmas." Cold, Eleanor, cold. She tried again. "I probably wouldn't see them again before Christmas even if I lived here!"

"I haven't seen the Anderson cousins in years," Rob

8

said. "Probably since Jeremy's wedding. Uncle Carl said we're welcome to come for a visit whenever we want."

Eleanor smiled gratefully at her oldest brother. "They're really nice." She turned to her mother. "Did you know I used to be afraid of him?"

"Afraid of Carl? Why on earth would you be afraid of Carl?"

"It was a long time ago, when we were on our way back from some family event. You said he didn't care about any children except his own. You were mad about it."

Kathy stared at her. "I never said any such thing."

"Yes, you did. I remember that," Rob interjected. "It was some political thing. He didn't support something you did, or you didn't support something he did. It was probably about homeschooling."

"Well, if I said that—and I don't remember it! —I didn't mean you should be afraid of him. He just sees certain things differently than we do. He has a limited view of the world, from up there in the country." In other words, they were all united in their enlightened views, and her brother was a backwoods hick.

This Thanksgiving, Eleanor was most devoutly grateful she'd been away from home over the election season.

"Anyhow, at Westerfield, you'd be able to substitute whenever you like, and you'd have a foot in the door when they hire for the new campus this summer." Kathy held up a hand to prevent interruption. "I know you want a break, but if you wait too long, you'll be set back another year. They'll have openings for every subject and grade level.

Eleanor broke off another forkful of pie. She didn't want to teach at all. She'd tried to tell her mother that, but she'd made the mistake of over-explaining it, talking too long, with not enough resolve.

"Westerfield's going to be in demand," her father said. "You'll do well to get in at the start."

"I'm going to stay up north." She hoped she didn't sound as desperate as she felt. She still had two days before she could go home. Back up north, away from her dear family.

"You won't like it up there for long," Zack said, "and you aren't getting any younger. You're going to want to be near Mom and Dad and the rest of us once you get married and have kids." He chucked Tyler under the chin. "You'd like a couple cousins, wouldn't you, fella?"

Zack and Laurie, having efficiently completed their family with only one pregnancy, had recently turned their attention to Eleanor's biological clock. They—and her other brothers and parents—had introduced her to a parade of teachers, politicians, and other suitable bachelors. She knew they meant well. They were genuinely concerned about her professional career and anxiously listening to that ticking clock. She ran a hundred miles away, and they could still hear it.

"Wouldn't it be fun if they had the same nanny?" Laurie asked.

Eleanor blinked. "The same nanny?"

"Well, when the twins are in school full-time, Ilse will be available."

"So," Eleanor said, "if I got married next month, got pregnant a few months later, had the baby and stayed home for at least a few months, that timing would work out for you?"

Laurie shook her head, not responding to the sarcasm. "Weddings take at least a year to plan, and the kids won't be in kindergarten for another two years." She sipped her coffee. "It was just a thought."

"Not to mention the fact that she doesn't have a boyfriend," Soren said, "but I suppose she could go ahead and start planning the wedding now."

"She's twenty-seven." Zack cut open a roll and spread cranberry butter on it. "She'd better start planning something."

"I don't need this." Eleanor stood, pushing her chair back. "I don't know if or when I'll get married, or if I'll have kids, but I've made one decision: I won't be returning to school in the fall. I am not going back to teaching." She almost enjoyed the moment of stunned silence. Even Tara, who'd been running a finger through the whipped cream on her pie, stopped and looked at her. "I don't know what I'm going to do, but I don't think I'm cut out to be a teacher."

"Not cut out..." Kathy Nielson's appalled voice trailed off.

"You're a good teacher," her father said. "Maybe you should look into high school or even college. Middle school can be rough."

"No, Dad. I'm just not good at it." She gestured widely, to encompass all of them. "That's you. Just because it's what you do, doesn't mean it's for me. I'm not like you."

"What else would you do?" Her mother asked.

"I don't know." She picked up her phone from the table and stuck it in her pocket. "I need some time to think about it."

11

They didn't give her time. They tag-teamed her, nagging and lecturing and reasoning, until she threatened to apply for a job as a Walmart greeter.

"You're a little overqualified for that," her mother said.

"I think I'd be rather good at it."

"I hope you're joking."

"Really," Eleanor insisted. "You say hello when they come in, help them with their carts, give stickers to the kids and then wave goodbye when they leave. It sounds like the perfect job."

Her mother reached out and caught Eleanor's hands. "Sweetheart, I'm sorry we've been pressuring you, but we just want the best for you. You are a good teacher, and it's important, meaningful work. You're making a difference in the lives of children. Investing in the future of America. The world!"

Was that supposed to be encouraging? It sounded like more pressure. "I don't think I was making a difference, Mom. I never felt like I was accomplishing anything at all. The world had better not count on me."

The older woman hesitated as if approaching a delicate topic. She shifted closer, still holding Eleanor's hands, and gazed into her eyes. "Your father and I have been talking. You've been going through a hard time, and maybe you should talk to someone. We'd be happy to pay for a counselor."

"Because I don't want to be a teacher?" Eleanor stood. "Come on, Mom... there are other careers in the world!"

Her mother's tender mood evaporated. "Maybe there are, but I don't see you pursuing any of them. You've just run off to find yourself, without thinking of anyone else."

Eleanor took a step forward. "I'm sorry, Mom. I'm not a teacher."

"Oh, Eleanor."

Their embrace felt hollow, as if nothing had been mended, but it had been an embrace. She wasn't leaving in an open quarrel. Hopefully, things would be better at Christmas. Or maybe there would be a blizzard, and she'd get snowed in at the cabin.

She should have listened to her mother. Eleanor leaned forward, clutching the steering wheel as if afraid it might jerk away and throw the Subaru Outback into the ditch. She'd left early enough to get home before dark, but at four o'clock, dusk hung in the trees. At least it wasn't snowing. A gray shadow flashed in her peripheral vision, and she flinched. She hadn't hit a deer since she was 18, but she still remembered the sick feeling.

The road narrowed to a tunnel, overhung with tree boughs, pines pressing in on both sides. Soren was right; she could get snowed in here. Uncle Gary said he'd keep it plowed, but what if there was a big storm or, like last year, new snow every day? She could never shovel her way out.

Relief lightened her spirits as she passed the sign and motion-activated floodlights lit the driveway. She'd become fond of that fish-shaped sign since moving here. Its incorrectly-placed apostrophe used to niggle at her, until her mother pointed out that since her brother was single, it was the proper usage. Currently single, her mother had clarified. Eleanor wondered if he kept a sign that said The

Andersons' in storage for his married phases.

She pulled into the garage and shut off the engine. She couldn't stay here through the winter. She'd be a basket case by December—even worse than she'd been six months ago, when she'd finally made the decision to leave her job and set out to find herself. She'd never find herself out here. She was lucky to find the cabin.

Cabin was a misnomer. Uncle Gary didn't seem to grasp the concept. This place was larger than his house in town and more luxuriously appointed. She tapped in the security code and pushed the door open. The hallway light came on automatically, flooding the great room with comfort. Through the glass wall of windows, security lights illuminated the backyard—front yard? Eleanor wasn't used to thinking of the road access as the backyard. The front yard was the one on the lake.

She switched off the exterior lights and went into the kitchen. In the evenings, now that it was dark so early, she felt exposed in the great room, with its massive glass wall. She preferred the interior spaces and the dining room, where blinds offered privacy from anyone skulking outside or on the lake.

Eleanor wrinkled her nose at the faint fragrance of cigar smoke. The refrigerator was probably full of beer, too, if her uncle and his friends hadn't drunk it all. He griped about city hunters who came up, drank themselves to sleep and then went out hung over, but he wasn't exactly abstinent himself. Eleanor cleared out for the long weekend, according to their agreement, so they could have their annual hunting trip. She hoped she wouldn't see deer carcasses hanging from trees in the morning.

They'd been tidy, at least. The furniture wasn't in quite the position she'd left it, and the mudroom was...

14

muddy. Cleaning was her responsibility—even cleaning up after a hunting party. Free rent came with a price.

The trill of her phone, unexpected in the silence, startled her. Her mother, of course. Eleanor picked up her coat and rummaged for the phone.

"Hi, Mom. I made it safely."

"Good! I've been worried. How was the trip?"

"Uneventful—the best kind."

"No deer? Was the traffic bad?"

"It was all going in the other direction. Hunters heading home with dead deer strapped to the tops of their SUV's. I had the northbound road to myself. And it's not exactly an expedition across the country." It sure felt like it, for the last 20 miles, though. Eleanor rolled the stiffness from her neck.

"Far enough, during hunting season, in the dark."

True. "Well, I just got here and dropped my bag in the hall. I'm going to put your care package in the fridge and get unpacked. I have work in the morning." She could hear her mother's disapproval in the brief silence. "It was fun to spend Thanksgiving with all of you. Tell Dad I love him and I'll beat him at chess when I'm there for Christmas."

"That reminds me." Her mother ignored Eleanor's attempt to end the conversation. "After you left, we started talking about our anniversary. Laurie wants to have a party for us."

"On Valentine's Day?"

"The fifteenth. Valentine's Day is on a Thursday. It was all her idea, but your dad and I are looking forward to it."

Her sister-in-law had jumped right into the Nielson family, not only adding another female to their male-dominated family but producing grandchildren. Twins. Laurie was an overachiever. Eleanor, still single with no prospects in sight, was a failure in more ways than one. It hadn't even occurred to her to throw a party. She would have called, of course, and maybe even remembered to send a card.

"That will be nice! I'll be there." They all knew she didn't have any other plans for Valentine's Day.

2

David Reid inhaled the cold air, welcoming the fresh bite after the clamor and heat of the gymnasium. Cars clogged the street, unloading returning students stuffed with turkey and hurrying back to cram for tomorrow's exams. There were always exams on the Monday after Thanksgiving weekend.

His own teachers were just as sadistic—he pictured them cackling and rubbing their hands in glee—but he'd come back in time to study before worship team practice on Friday. It was his turn to choose the songs, and he'd sneaked in one of his Russ Taff favorites. Not many of today's congregation had known it, of course, but the "Praise the Lord' choruses were easy to pick up. The older members of the church—the Jesus People generation—sang it with gusto.

"Hey, David!"

He turned and waited for his friend. "Hey, Larry. What are you doing out here?"

The other man trotted to catch up. Not built for trotting, he puffed at the exertion as he came to a stop. "Hoping to find you. I texted a couple times, then I called, and left a voice message, and then I remembered you were here and probably had your phone in a locker. I was afraid you'd get all of it at once and think it was an emergency, so

I thought I'd run over and talk to you at the gym."

David chuckled. "But it's not an emergency?"

"Not really an emergency—not for me, anyhow. Cal asked me to ask you to take the presentation to the city council tomorrow because his daughter had her baby early, and he and Meg are flying out there."

"He asked you to ask me...." His boss was notorious for sliding out of awkward situations. "Are his daughter and the baby okay?"

"I think so. He was in a hurry and asked me if I'd talk to you. He said you knew all about the proposal and could present it as well as he could."

"You do know I have to wear a suit and tie for that, right?" David asked darkly.

Larry sighed, looking like a deflating balloon. "Sorry."

"Not your fault." David slapped him on the back. "Cal does that—makes other people do the dirty work. He should have called me himself, but there you were... all sympathetic and wanting to be helpful. He's an engineer, not a people person like you."

"That's me... a psychologist has to be a people person."

"Hey, it pays well, right? And there's job security. The world gets crazier all the time, so psychologists will always be in demand."

Larry scratched his nose. "That's not exactly how it's supposed to work. Do you need a ride home?"

"That would be great, thanks. I'd better review the proposal and iron my good shirt."

David ran a finger around the inside of his collar. Associate pastors didn't have to wear dress shirts and ties, did they? These days, even head pastors dressed more casually. As an engineer, he usually wore whatever was clean and comfortable. It was a good job—just not his calling.

This had been a futile attempt, just like the last one, and just like the next one would be. Cal's technology was miles ahead of everyone else, but he couldn't back up his claims with years of successful application, and no one would give him the opportunity to try. The city council members were interested and liked the proposal; they just couldn't put taxpayer money into something that might or might not work. When they did, Ridgewell Mechanical would be ready to go. They'd bring big jobs to the community, too—big for St. Cloud, anyhow.

He tugged the tie loose and shoved it into the pocket of his wool coat, his fingers touching his cell phone just as it vibrated. He answered without reading the screen.

"David Reid, Ridgewell Mechanical."

"Hello, David. I'm so glad I caught you!"

Angela. He'd let her last few attempts go to voice mail, feeling guilty for not answering her calls but conflicted about how to respond.

"Hi, Angela. Sorry I missed your calls. It's been hectic." He glanced back at the building he'd just left. "I'm at city hall right now, working. Is there something I can do for you?" Wrong question. He tried to think of an excuse, but she jumped in ahead of him.

"How about lunch? Engineers have to eat, to keep that brain fueled up." Her tone was flirtatious. "Or if you're stuck at work like you usually are, how about dinner? At my place, or we can go out."

"I have classes most evenings." He'd told her that a dozen times. He softened his voice. After all, she knew he was a Christian. He ought to be winning her for Christ, not driving her off. "It's just a busy time for me."

"Not too busy to eat," she insisted. "We could grab a bite right after you get off work."

"I can't." He tried to sound regretful. Cal's much-younger sister was like a bulldozer. She'd already driven over two of his coworkers, and he was the next man in her path. David had no desire to join her list of victims.

"What about Sunday? I'd love to visit your church, and we could have brunch afterward."

He stopped and pulled the phone away from his ear, staring at the screen as if he could read her mind through it. Surely, she had no desire to go to church. She was probably just willing to sit through 90 minutes of boredom if it would get her what she wanted. Right now, that appeared to be David.

Church. She'd found the golden ticket. He couldn't say no to taking her to church.

"Okay, do you know where Grace Chapel is?" David held the phone between his ear and shoulder while he buttoned his coat.

"How about if you just pick me up?"

Oh, no. That wasn't happening. "I have to be there early. Really early, for music practice and prayer meeting."

"Prayer meeting? Is that open to the public? I could do that."

He grinned at the optimistic note in her voice. Under different circumstances, he'd admire her persistence. "It's really just a small group of guys—mostly older men. The service starts at ten."

"Sounds good! I don't know anyone there, so I'll sit

with you."

The old ladies of the church would eat that up. They were always trying to introduce him to their granddaughters and nieces, convinced that a single man with a steady job must be in want of a wife. So far, none of the granddaughters and nieces had been at all interested in becoming a wife.

"And we'll go out for brunch afterward," Angela finished triumphantly. "See you then, David!"

Maybe Pastor Jack would have a good sermon on Sunday. Something scholarly that David could expound upon through brunch. He'd bore her into abandoning him. Guiltily, he winced as he slid the phone back into his pocket with the despised necktie. Jack did like to preach Old Testament exposition, but it would be better to have an evangelical message for Angela. How could he be so self-centered and conceited? That girl needed Jesus.

The phone rang again almost immediately, and he checked the caller name before answering.

"Hi, Mom."

"Hello! I just called to see how your presentation went. Any luck?"

"Nope, another rejection. My ego is suffering."

She chuckled. "I doubt it. It'll happen eventually, even if it's after you're gone."

He headed toward the parking lot, glad to have a normal conversation after what he could only describe as an assault. "Hey, you want to come to church with me this weekend?"

"I don't think we can, this weekend. Is something special going on?"

"No, just wondering."

"How about next weekend? We could do that."

David opened his car door and climbed inside. Out of the wind, he relaxed in the sun-warmed interior. "I bet you just need a weekend to recover from Thanksgiving."

"Well, your dad did suggest a vacation was in order. That was quite a day."

"There must have been a hundred kids," David said. "All of my cousins are reproducing like rabbits."

His mother laughed. "No one person had more than two or three kids... there are just a lot of you! We've never had everyone from both sides of the family all at once before—at least, not since you were little. And it wasn't a hundred kids."

"It seemed like it."

"There were 13," she said, "and Ian is 16, so you really shouldn't count him with the children. But five of them were under five years old, and it was pretty hectic."

It had been great. David spent most of Thanksgiving Day playing games with the older kids and tickling the little ones. He looked out the windshield. A young woman waited at the intersection, pushing a stroller and holding another child by the hand. The little girl was hopping up and down and appeared to be singing. "Maybe you'll have a grandchild of your own next year, if Nick and Heather finally get around to starting a family."

"Maybe."

"I was looking at all those kids," David said, "and I realized that none of them are Reids. I'm the only Reid descendant. Grandpa Ken was the only boy in his family. Uncle Kenneth had all girls."

"That's right. Does that worry you?"

"I just hadn't thought about it. I also realized that I'm the only unmarried cousin on either side of our family, Except for Uncle Kenneth's girls, and they're all still in school." Everyone was paired off in happy couples, families with babies and full lives. David, the thirty-year-old engineer, was still single. Loser.

"You'll find the right girl in God's timing, David. Right now, you're pretty busy with work and school."

"But I don't think there's ever going to be a time when I'm not busy. You're busy, and all your kids are grown and gone."

"That's true," she agreed, "but it will happen, David. Yes, we'd love to have grandchildren, but we'll be grateful for whatever God sends us. On Thanksgiving, He sent us 13 great-nieces and nephews, and that was a bit overwhelming."

"It sure was." David started the car. "I need to get back to work, so I'll talk to you later. Plan on next Sunday, though. Love you."

"I love you, too. Be careful."

"I always am. Don't forget next Sunday."

At least he'd have backup if Angela wanted to attend the following weekend, too.

3

I don't know if you saw the weather forecast or not, but we're supposed to get some snow tonight."

Gary Anderson, a lanky man with the blue eyes and prominent brow of his Scandinavian ancestors, peered at Eleanor over the reading glasses he wore in the office.

Her heart sank. "How much?"

"Just a few inches. Maybe three. Do you want me to come and plow you out in the morning?"

She shook her head. "I'm sure it'll be fine. The Outback has all-wheel drive. I'm a Minnesotan, remember? We can drive in snow."

"You can drive in city snow," her uncle retorted. "Have you ever been out of town in the snow? A little wind can drift the snow right over the road, and it's hard not to slam on the brakes when something jumps out in front of you. That's when accidents happen."

"I know not to slam on the brakes and to watch for other cars that may not be able to stop at intersections. I'm sure I'll be fine if I go slowly."

"I'll come out and plow, just to make sure. Better safe than sorry."

He went into his office, and Eleanor spun on her stool, tapping the blueprints she'd been examining. He wouldn't like having to plow all the way to the cabin every time it snowed this winter. Last year, they'd had three feet of snow in April. She could shovel, or even learn to use the snowblower Uncle Gary kept in the garage, but the road to the cabin was a mile long and not high on the county's plowing priority list.

She couldn't afford to move. The use of the cabin was part of her pay. Even if Uncle Gary was willing to pay her a bit more, rentals were scarce. And why should he pay her more? She was slow as molasses at her job, and he had to double-check everything she did. The last take-off had been perfect, though, and she was studying the manuals he'd given her. She'd get better.

The work absorbed her attention. It was like a puzzle. The answers were right or wrong, unlike teaching, with its subjective nature and results that might not be seen for years—if she was making a difference at all.

Three hours later, Eleanor stretched and slid from the stool. Lunchtime. Peanut butter and jelly were good for you, right? It had been one of her favorite lunches, when it was a special treat instead of a steady diet. For the last few years, she'd wolfed down microwaved frozen meals and hurried back to her classroom to prepare for her next class—and to make sure the dear children didn't come in and steal her stapler.

Her uncle looked up as she passed his desk. "How's it going in there?"

"Good! The electrical is the hardest part, and I'm nearly done with that."

"Great. Can you do me a favor after lunch?"

"Sure." She'd gladly be his girl Friday if it meant he could keep her employed. There wasn't a lot of work in the winter, for his construction company or anyone else in the area.

"I've got some old blueprints for Aunt Violet. I have no idea what she wants them for, but I don't need them. Can you bring them out to her at the farmhouse?"

"I haven't seen the farmhouse since she moved back there," Eleanor said. "I wonder if Penny will be there. I haven't seen her in ages."

"Maybe. Your uncle Carl said she's there nearly every day." He shook his head. "I don't know how well a bridal shop will do all the way out there."

"It'll be fine. Penny's a smart woman."

"Mmhm. I hope that's enough."

No one appeared to be home. Eleanor considered the old farmhouse from the comfortable warmth of her car. Her only memories of the place were of kittens she'd found in the barn and playing shadow tag with her cousins. The barn was gone now. The driveway was paved, with a little parking area and a walkway that curved around the house, rising gently and ending at a side door. An elegantly-disguised wheelchair ramp. Uncle Carl's landscaping business at work, no doubt. The yard, sparse and frozen, would be beautiful when he finished it in the spring.

The gray and white house managed to look contemporary without denying its farmhouse roots. The blue door—not the ubiquitous red—gave it distinction. Still... would brides really drive all the way out from the cities to get their dresses made by an unknown young woman with no credentials? In a farmhouse?

Eleanor put the car in gear. She'd drop off the blueprints at the Andersons' house after work. Maybe she could catch Penny or Violet there. She hadn't seen any of them yet. Aunt Connie's invitation to Thanksgiving dinner, delivered through Uncle Gary, had been a matter of form. They knew she had to go home. Now, she wished she'd accepted.

A red car whipped into the parking lot even as Eleanor started to back up, a blond girl emerging, waving, almost before the car stopped.

"Hi! Did you have an appointment with Penny? She's running late. She got a flat tire and didn't have a spare, so her aunt and the handyman went out to help her. Can you wait?"

Eleanor opened the car door. "No appointment. I'm her cousin. I just came to drop off some stuff for Aunt Violet."

"Oh, it's nice to meet you! I'm Brittany. I do Penny's marketing and social media."

"Eleanor Nielson. I just moved here. I haven't even seen Penny in years. Aunt Violet, either."

"Violet will be back in a few minutes."

On cue, a blue Buick turned in and parked on the other side of Brittany's car. Eleanor hurried to meet her. Aunt Violet didn't look any different than she had last time Eleanor had seen her. Thin, with snow white hair and faded blue eyes, she leaned on a cane as she rose from the car. There was something very comforting about elderly relatives. They made her feel like she had roots. An odd thought, but true.

"Nellie!"

An unexpected lump grew in Eleanor's throat as Violet embraced her. No one else had ever called her that—fortunately—and even though she'd never been close to her aunt before, she felt like she'd come home.

"Nellie Nielson! That's a terrible name," Eleanor said. "I used to get called Ellie sometimes, but Mom's always said Eleanor, and it stuck."

"I called you Nellie when you were a baby," the older woman said. "You were a sweet little thing, with big blue eyes and always waving your arms around."

"Mom says that's how she knew I'd be good at volleyball. I've got some blueprints for you, from Uncle Gary. Can you show me around? I'd love to see what you've done here."

"The main part of the house is Penny's, but you can see my little home in the annex."

"I'm going to wait in my car for Penny," Brittany said. "I've got some calls to make. It was nice to meet you!"

"Yes, nice to meet you, too." Eleanor shook hands with the girl.

"I'm sure we'll meet again."

That would be nice. She could use a few friends here. Eleanor grabbed the rolls of paper and followed her aunt to a back door. "So, are you all moved in? Penny's going to live upstairs, over her shop, right?"

"Not yet." Violet twisted a key in the lock and pushed the door open. "We're moving in at the beginning of the year, but then I'm leaving at the beginning of February, for Florida. I'll stay with your grandma and Aunt Colleen until the weather improves."

"That's a good plan." Eleanor shivered dramatically. She looked around the spacious kitchen. "This is nice. Is this where Mom lived when she was little?"

"Oh, yes, she did. I'll make some coffee."

It would be rude to leave right away. Eleanor shrugged out of her coat and hung it on the rack. Uncle Gary wouldn't mind.

Violet talked while she filled an old-fashioned percolator coffee maker. "It's plenty big for me. I'll have two rooms for my sewing. One's just an ordinary sewing room, and the other will have the long-arm quilting machine in it. That leaves me with one bedroom for myself and a spare. Would you like a look around while the water boils?"

"Yes! You have four bedrooms here?"

"They were always full, until we all left and closed the place up. We even had some boarders for a while, but then it was abandoned until we decided to put the bridal shop in here." Violet looked around with satisfaction. "Now it's all mine—this part, anyhow, and that's enough for me."

"So, you've come home." The idea was... heartwarming.

"Yes, I have. But it's the people who matter, you know, and I was always with family." Violet pushed a door open. "This was the master bedroom, but I'm putting the quilting machine in there. The previous owner will be here tomorrow to assemble it for me."

"That makes quilts?" The electrical equipment and metal pieces, including several long pipes, looked like something from one of Uncle Gary's work sites.

"It quilts them. A great improvement over doing them by hand. This room opposite is mine, and that's the sewing room."

She pointed, and Eleanor obediently moved to look inside. It didn't exactly look like a tornado had gone through it, since everything was still piled up, but she wondered how her aunt could accomplish anything in such a jumble. The rest of the house was so clean and orderly.

"I keep most of my material and other supplies in totes in the laundry room. It used to be a sort of mudroom, but now it's just laundry. I was going to keep them in that room at the end of the hall, but your uncle Carl said I should keep it for guests." She sniffed. "I suppose your grandma might come, but she'd stay with them, especially now that I'm moving out and they'll have more room. But Brian—Penny's young man—fixed up a lot of shelves in the laundry room, and I didn't want to hurt his feelings."

Violet turned back toward the kitchen, and Eleanor followed. "I saw you have patio furniture out back. It'll be a nice place to sit when it gets warmer."

"We used to sit out there, a long time ago, before all those trees got too big and blocked the view." She opened a cupboard and took out cups and saucers. "I have some sandbakkels, too. Do you like those?"

"I don't know. What are they?"

"Cookies! Swedish cookies. Doesn't your mother make them?"

Eleanor shook her head. "She makes sugar cookies and gingerbread men at Christmastime. And sometimes others, but I don't think I've heard of sandbakkels."

"Hmph. She used to love making sandbakkels, even when it wasn't Christmas. Have a seat."

Eleanor sat. It was odd to hear of her mother spoken of as a child, so casually, by this woman who was nearly a stranger. "Then I'm sure I'll enjoy them. Can I help with anything?"

"No, it's all done." Violet set the filled cups on the

table and returned for a plate of cookies. "Penny will want to show you the rest of the house herself. She's been working hard on it." She transferred a cookie to her plate. "The annex will do nicely for me."

"It's larger than I thought," Eleanor said, "but it still seems cozy. The cabin is so big and empty. It's strange to be there alone at night. I've been playing music, like white noise, to drown out the wind and coyotes."

Instead of filling the house with warmth, though, the music made it worse. If it was quiet, it disappeared, swallowed up in the vastness of the great room. When she turned up the volume, it echoed off the walls and ceiling.

Aunt Violet frowned. "All by yourself. I don't like that. Are you driving back and forth every day?"

"Yes, for now." Eleanor took a cautious sip of the black coffee. "I'm a little worried about winter. Uncle Gary says he'll plow, but he's so busy."

"And he's not going to plow you all the way to town! What if the power goes out or your car breaks down? Or if there's a lot of snow and he can't get out, either?"

Eleanor blinked. "You aren't exactly reassuring me, Aunt Violet."

"Has anyone ever lived there over the winter before?"

"I don't know," Eleanor said, "but Uncle Gary said it's all winterized. It's not exactly a rustic cabin. It's bigger than my parents' house and a lot nicer."

"It's a cabin, and isolated. What would you do in an emergency?" Violet snapped. "That boy doesn't have a lick of sense. Why are you staying out there?"

"I... It's sort of a perk of the job. I'm not all that helpful at the office, so I don't expect a lot of money. If I stay at the cabin, I don't have to pay rent or utilities."

Her aunt narrowed her eyes speculatively. "You're keeping it clean and lived in. Empty houses are a target for bugs and rodents and vandals. You're doing him a favor."

"No, not really. It's a beautiful place. I'm grateful." She ran a finger around the cup's handle. "It's just a bit remote, and with winter coming, it does make me nervous. But it'll be fine." She took a bite of cookie, mostly to put an end to her protests.

"I don't like the idea of you all alone out there. Why don't you get a place of your own, in town?"

"I've been thinking about it. I'll check the buy-sell-trade groups on Facebook. Maybe someone wants a roommate." Eleanor sighed. Just like college. The garage apartment her parents fixed up for her was nice, but it wasn't like being independent. She'd stayed long enough to pay off the student loans, and then, instead of looking for a place of her own, she ran away and ended up in a remote cabin without a real job.

"I don't care for the sound of that at all." Violet set her cup down, clinking against the saucer. "You're going to meet up with someone online and live with them?"

"I'd ask for references," Eleanor said meekly. "Or at least I could look for rentals cheap enough to get without a roommate."

"You can move in with me." The offer sounded more like a declaration. A command.

Eleanor bit her lip. Living in the back bedroom at her elderly aunt's house was a step in the opposite direction of independence. At least she had privacy at the cabin. "I don't know... I didn't mean to put you on the spot. The cabin is so luxurious. Even if I was snowed in for a day or two, I'd be comfortable. There's even a wood-burning stove in the rec room downstairs, in case the heat goes out."

"You know how to use a wood stove?"

"I'll get Uncle Gary to show me." Eleanor smiled at her aunt. "Really, I'm fine. Have you been out there? It's like a resort."

"No, I haven't. I know cabins, though, even nice ones, and they're still cabins."

"You could come out and stay with me," Eleanor teased. "At least until you're ready to move in here."

"No, thank you. I'd rather move in here now, but Carl doesn't like the idea of me being here alone. I wonder if he knows you're alone out at the cabin."

Her uncle Carl wouldn't worry about Eleanor falling and breaking a hip, though. Someone as frail as Aunt Violet should be closer to other people, in case of emergency. She stood up. "I'd better get back to work before Uncle Gary docks my pay."

Her aunt didn't move. "I don't understand what you're doing for him, anyhow. I thought you were a teacher. Didn't you get a master's degree? Sit down."

Eleanor complied. "I decided to try something else for a while."

Violet gave an unladylike snort. "Working for a construction company?"

"I'm actually enjoying it. One of the things I'm doing is taking off project plans. That means I go through the blueprints or plans and make a list of all the items we'd need to buy to build the project." She pressed a finger against the cookie crumbs and licked it clean. "I know it sounds dumb, but it's kind of satisfying. I figure out how many eight-foot, 6-inch pipes we need, and how many six-inch, ninety-degree flanged elbows and how many bolts it would take to join all of the pipes. Or electrical wiring and outlets. That's more complicated, but I'm getting it."

"But you're a teacher!" Her aunt didn't sound impressed with her new skills. "You sound like Brian, with your wiring."

"Brian?"

"Penny's young man. The one who set up my storage. He's been re-doing all the electrical work and anything else he can think of, as an excuse to hang around."

"Oh. Well, I don't know anything about electricity—just adding up the length of wires and components. Same with the rest of it. I'm in the office, not out doing the work."

Violet tipped her head to one side. "If you come now, Carl couldn't have any objection to me moving in early. And it would be safer for you than living out at the lake."

Eleanor looked at her. She didn't want to be manipulated. She'd just run away from that and was enjoying the freedom. "I don't think I can. I've made a commitment to Uncle Gary. And like you said, the house shouldn't be left empty. If I get snowed in, I'll do a lot of reading and be cozy in front of the wood stove. It sounds kind of fun."

It sounded terrifying. The cabin was more cavernous than cozy, with its prow front wall of windows, massive stone fireplace, and high ceilings that peaked at twenty feet. The logs were bigger than any pine tree she'd ever seen.

"Well, I think you'll be ready to move to town sooner than later." The old lady stared at her for a few seconds. "In fact, you could be helpful to me."

"Helpful?"

"I've been working on some little books, to go with my family history quilts. I thought they were good, but I started rereading them a few months ago, and they're terrible. They need an English teacher to go over them. Editing. There are some that still need to be typed up, since I didn't have a typewriter or computer when I started."

"You write books to go with quilts?" Interested, Eleanor sipped her coffee. It was cold.

"I make family history quilts. Didn't your mother tell you?"

"Um, no. She didn't mention it." Why hadn't she? Eleanor was beginning to wonder if she knew her mother at all.

"I've been making them for years. At least fifty years. Penny says they're like a scrapbook. I write books—stories, anyhow—to go with them, to explain what they are and why I did different things with them. I could use your help with that."

And move in early. Yep, Eleanor recognized manipulation when she saw it. "I don't think I should, right now. Would you be willing to keep the offer open for a while, in case it does get too hard out there? And if I did move in," she added hastily, "it would be temporary, while I look for a place of my own." She reached across the table and patted the blue-veined hand. "But thank you."

4

D id you hear Jack say that the church is booked with weddings every Saturday this month?"

"You wouldn't think January would be a big month for weddings in Minnesota." Larry paused, his cup halfway to his mouth. "But it's cold and dark, so maybe people are looking for a partner then. One person can't stay warm alone, you know."

"No," David said, "it doesn't work like that. According to my sister and cousins, weddings take at least a year to plan. It's ridiculous. Once you get engaged, you should just get married."

"I heard that. One of my clients is engaged. Her wedding is over a year away, and she's in a constant state of anxiety about it."

"Why? The wedding or the marriage? Don't get me wrong, Larry, but if my bride was so stressed out by the wedding that she had to see a psychologist, I'd wonder if she really wanted to marry me. And how would she do with married life?" David demanded, warming to his topic. "And kids?"

Larry shrugged. "Don't know."

"And a year! Larry, I'm thirty. If I found a girl tomorrow, dated for at least a few months before proposing and then had to wait a year to get married, I'd be nearly thirty-two. And even if we start a family right away, I'd probably be 33 or so when the first one is born. If we have two or three..." He broke off, offended. "What are you laughing at?"

"Only an engineer would do the math like that."

"I want to have a family, and I want to do it young enough that I can enjoy my retirement with an empty nest."

Larry chuckled again, getting his whole body involved. "In other words, you want to have kids and get it over with, skipping all the parenting years, and enjoy the grandchildren."

David grinned. "That's not exactly what I meant, but my folks are in their fifties, and Heather and I have been out of the house for ten years. They're done with kids and seem to be enjoying themselves. My aunt and uncle are nearly sixty and still have two daughters in college and one who's a high school senior. I'd like to have my kids while I'm young enough to enjoy them—and enjoy life after they're grown and gone, too."

"But babies don't come on a schedule—at least, not usually—and you're not married yet. You don't even have a girlfriend. I've never even known you to have a date."

"Thanks for making me feel good, Larry." David pointed his fork at his friend. "I don't see girls hanging on you, either."

"Nope." Larry scowled at the grapefruit wedges on his plate. "I'm not good husband material right now. The doctor said if I don't lose at least fifty pounds, this might be my last birthday. I'll either have a heart attack or get diabetes."

"You're doing great. You didn't cave to peer pressure and order French toast." David ran the last piece of sugar-dusted bread through a puddle of lingonberry syrup.

His friend eyed the morsel with regret. "I don't have a death wish. The weight just piled on, a bit at a time, and the doctor says that's what it'll keep doing unless I make drastic changes. So, grapefruit and celery are my new best friends. I'm getting a gym membership, too."

"Good for you." David returned to their previous conversation. "I've had a few dates, set up by the matchmaking grannies at church, but none of them clicked." He set his fork on his plate and pushed it toward the edge of the table. "I don't even know any girls. I'm too old for college students."

"I know what you mean." Larry nodded. "I get older and they get younger every year."

"Right now, after a family Christmas that looked like something out of Norman Rockwell, I feel like everyone around me has this wonderful life and I'm sitting at home alone. Everyone else my age is married with a family."

"Except me," Larry said. "You really feel strongly about this. I'm sorry I laughed."

"It's okay. I'm just feeling sorry for myself after the holidays. Everyone says to wait... that God will bring me the perfect wife, but I'm not sure that means I should sit home, waiting for her to show up on my doorstep. We don't have any women in the office, and there aren't any single young women at church. My seminary classes are online. I don't know where I'd meet the right kind of woman."

"Oh! Hold on." Larry reached for his coat and dug into the pocket. "I just saw something this morning on Facebook. It's a new matchmaking company."

"Oh, no." David shook his head. "I'm not doing online dating. I've heard too many horror stories, even from those Christian sites."

"It's the way everyone meets people these days. I know several people who met online."

"Not me."

"I don't think this one's like a regular dating site." Larry flicked his finger against the screen, scrolling through posts. "It sounded more like people looking for relationships, not dating. You can get a professional matchmaker."

"Matchmaker. A professional matchmaker? Is there a college degree for that?"

"Didn't you tell me you did Fiddler on the Roof in community theater? There was a matchmaker in that." Larry continued his search. "I wish I could remember the name of the company."

"Yenta?" David scoffed. "Is she on Facebook now?"

"Here it is. Betwixt Two Hearts. There. I shared it with you."

"You didn't post it on my page, did you?" David picked up his own phone, alarmed. "I can just imagine what my family would say. They're ruthless."

"No, I sent a message. See?" Larry held up his phone. "Computer-matching or a personal matchmaker. Not professional."

"I'm not interested in computer dating."

"Look at it. You can tell them what you want. So, tell them you want a wife."

Exasperated, David dropped the phone face-down on the table. "Like ordering one from Amazon? A modern version of mail-order brides?"

Larry shrugged. "Or like Abraham, sending his

servants out to find a wife for Isaac. It says here you fill out a questionnaire and they match you up with someone. You don't go through a list of people like you do on those other websites."

"I think I'll just wait for a real girl. Woman."

"How long you gonna wait?" Larry leaned back, still reading the website. "You might have kids at home till you're eighty. If you get any at all."

"I'm not that desperate."

Larry peered over the phone, brows raised. "Really? I saw Angela at church a few weeks ago. I wasn't going to mention it, but..."

"What am I supposed to do? Tell her she can't come to church? I think she's given up on me, though. We went out to brunch afterward and I told her I'm in school to be a pastor. She wasn't impressed." He slid from the booth. "I've got to get going. Happy birthday. Hope you enjoyed your grapefruit and yogurt."

"Thanks. But really, man, it's okay to check this out. Everyone's doing it. It's hard to meet people once you're out of college or in a church like ours, where almost everyone's over 40 or already married. Someday..." Larry patted his stomach. "I may just look into it for myself, once I've got in shape. No girl's going to look at me like this."

"The right girl will. You probably won't find her on a dating website, though."

"That's awesome." David watched the ball spin, spiraling around the pole. It had a hypnotic effect, probably because of its silence as it traveled up and down.

"But I'm getting dizzy watching it. Did you have any practical application in mind, or is it just for fun?"

His boss smirked. "Just for fun, so far, but I'll find something to do with it. Some of my best machines started out as toys." He pointed the controller and the ball fell to the floor.

"Now you can make toys for your grandson," David said. "He must be about six weeks old now, right? Did you know they make Tinker Toys for babies?"

"Really?" Cal tapped his watch and raised it to his face. "Tinker Toys."

"Are you making a Christmas shopping list already?"

"Mostly Legos, so far. Meg likes to add things like baby dolls and teddy bears, just to pull my chain. She says he'll need lots of warm fuzzies to compensate for the engineering gene."

"She might have a point. Has she forgiven you for the vacuum system you gave her for your anniversary?"

Cal hunched his shoulders. "It was a great design. She could use it for everything, even things she drops down the drain, like the cap from the tube of toothpaste, or for getting the crumbs under the heating element in the oven. I made a dozen specialized attachments, all personalized just for her."

"And she didn't think that was romantic?" David smiled sympathetically. Cal had spent weeks on that, ignoring the warnings of his friends, determined to make it a perfect, one-of-a-kind gift for his wife. It was a true labor of love, the most romantic thing Cal could think of, and after twenty-five years of marriage, Meg ought to have understood that.

"Not really, but she's using it, or makes me use it.

I'd have been in real trouble if Angela hadn't been there."

"Angela?"

"Yeah, she dragged me aside, forced me to give her my credit card, and came back an hour later—still during the party—with a diamond bracelet. A very expensive diamond bracelet, in a gift-wrapped box and a card signed with my name. She told Meg the vacuum cleaner was just a joke, and this was her real gift."

"I didn't hear that part." Angela probably knew her brother pretty well.

Cal rubbed the back of his neck. "I'm not sure she believed it. She loves the bracelet, though, and she says I should shop at that store for all her gifts from now on."

"That will simplify your shopping," David said, concealing a smile.

"But it's so impersonal," Cal complained. "Meg's the most amazing woman in the world, and it seems kind of cold to just buy jewelry instead of making her something really special." He regarded his invention. "This would make a great mobile for a baby. You'd have to keep it out of their reach and make sure the batteries don't die. I should ask Meg about it."

David watched him wander in the direction of his office, already talking to his wife through the blue-tooth earpiece. That, with all its weirdness, was what he wanted in a marriage. Cal adored his wife, convinced she was even more brilliant than he—with his genius IQ—would ever be. To him, Meg was the most beautiful, desirable woman in the world. Meg, despite her reaction to the vacuum cleaner, loved her husband. She laughed at his jokes and teased him about the baby gifts. Cal was an odd duck. Meg saw that and liked it. She didn't try to change him into someone else.

They'd been high school sweethearts. She'd supported him in their early years, working so he could go to college and then start his own business instead of taking a high-paying job in another company. As soon as Cal made his first big sale, she quit her job to become a full-time wife and mother. They were living happily—if a bit strangely—ever after.

He caught his reflection in the glass wall. He was a nice, ordinary-looking guy. Clean, polite, kind to children and small animals... Not nearly as odd as Cal, but Cal had a great marriage, and David was single. Why hadn't he had the foresight to get a high school sweetheart?

Brittany breezed through the door of the coffee shop just as Eleanor ended the phone call. How did the girl do it? Eleanor couldn't breeze through a doorway to save her life, but it looked natural on Brittany. Brittany had flair. Style. Personality.

"Hi, there. Sorry I'm late. You already got your coffee?"

Eleanor raised her cup. "I was freezing."

"It's cold out." Brittany tilted her head, concern creasing her brow. "Is something wrong?"

Perceptive, too. Eleanor took a sip of the too-hot coffee before responding. "No, I'm fine. I was just talking to my sister-in-law. She's throwing a party for my parents' anniversary."

"That's nice." Brittany tugged off heavy mittens and shoved them into her coat pockets. "How long have they been married?"

"Thirty-five years. It's not even like it's fifty or something! Why do they need such a big deal for their thirty-fifth?"

"Um... I don't know. Thirty-five years is a long time, and it's always fun to have a party." Brittany pointed. "There's an empty table."

Eleanor slid onto a stool. "But this is a big party, and way more... fancy than I expected. She's having a string quartet and a wine bar!"

Brittany's mouth fell open. "A wine bar? Is that like an open bar with just wine? No beer or mixed drinks?"

"I think so. And she's meeting with a caterer to taste finger foods that will cost more than a sit-down meal." Eleanor propped her chin on her hand, elbow precariously near her cup. "Laurie can afford it, but still... it's their thirty-fifth. An accomplishment, no doubt, but still..."

"Let me get something to drink, and you can tell me about it. It sounds like fun."

Not fun. Eleanor watched her new friend chat with the barista. Her unexpected friendship with Brittany was one of the best things in her life here. It reminded her of college days, when no one expected anything of her except that she do her schoolwork and be a friend.

Brittany set her coffee on the table and shrugged out of her coat before settling on the other stool. "So, this party... what are you going to wear? Can you sew like Penny?"

"I don't know. I mean, no, I don't sew, and I don't know what I'm going to wear." Would Brittany understand? Their friendship hadn't progressed to the soul-baring level yet.

"You don't look very happy about it."

"It's just... the thing is, Laurie expects me to come

with a date. They all expect it."

"Oh. Is that a problem? I suppose it's down in the cities. Do you know someone down there to invite? It might be awkward to ask someone from up here, especially if you have to spend the night." Brittany leaned forward. "Do you really need a date? I mean, they know you'll be driving in from out of town.

"I don't think they care about that. They expect a date. A good one."

"A good one?" Brittany's eyes widened.

"Someone presentable, preferably a professional of some kind," Eleanor said. "Someone who fits in with their crowd. And preferably someone who will convince me to return to civilization and get a real job."

"Wow." Brittany stopped stirring sugar into her coffee and stared. "That's... interesting. I didn't realize your parents were so different from Penny's."

"Totally different. It's hard to believe they're related. Uncle Carl and Gary are so down to earth. My mother acts like they're backwoods hicks. But she grew up here, too." The words burst out on their own.

"She's their sister, right? Will they be invited to the party?"

"Probably. They might even go." A happy thought occurred to Eleanor. "Maybe Aunt Violet will go, and I can say she's my date. I need to take care of her, so I can't have a man tagging along."

"Your aunt isn't that frail, and she'll whap you with her cane if you imply she is."

"True. If I carpooled down there with some of the family, I wouldn't need a date," Eleanor mused, "but it would be better if I had a date."

"But you don't?"

"No. The thing is, when she started talking about table arrangements and invitations, Laurie assumed I'd be bringing a 'plus one.' I didn't correct her. It kind of snowballed, and now everyone is looking forward to meeting my date." She hadn't exactly lied... she just hadn't corrected them. "If I have a date, maybe they'll believe I have a real life up here."

"You do have a life up here! You said you like your job, and you've got family here." She flashed a bright smile. "And a friend."

That did sound like a real life. "Thanks."

"They just want you closer to home?" Brittany asked.

"Sort of. They do, but it's more than that. I need some time to decide what I want to do." Eleanor smiled tightly. "What I want to do when I grow up. I just always assumed I would do the same things they do. I was born to be a teacher. But now, I'm not sure. Or rather, I'm pretty sure I'm not a teacher. I quit my job and came up here to find myself."

"Okay, but it's not like you backpacked to Tibet. You're only an hour away, in your mom's home town, and you got a job with your uncle. You're surrounded by family."

She didn't get it. Eleanor tried to find words that wouldn't make her parents sound like conceited snobs. "Mom and Dad believe in what they do. They think it's so important that nothing else really matters. Their friends are all like them or are in a position to help them—usually in politics. It's not that they look down on people like Uncle Carl and Gary. They just sort of see them as... outsiders." She shrugged. "They raised my brothers and me to follow in their footsteps. Sports and education. Music lessons, the right social activities. I was a member of the same sorority my mom was, even if I did go to an out-of-state school."

Brittany looked fascinated. "I had no idea. I assumed you were like everyone else here. I mean, like Penny and her siblings."

"I am! I'm making them sound bad, but my parents are great people. They're involved in every kind of charity, especially for education. My brothers, too. They're all teachers or started as teachers. Really good people." Eleanor's cheeks burned with embarrassment. "I'm the one who didn't fit in."

"And if you go back without a date, you'll be answering questions and they'll feel sorry for you. And probably pressuring you to move back there, I suppose." She sipped her coffee. "There must be someone in the area who'd go with you. Didn't you have a boyfriend there? You said you lived there for three years after college."

"I did, twice, but nothing ever came of it. They were both nice guys. Mom and Dad approved of both of them, and it was convenient to have a date for things," Eleanor said. "In the end, both times, I got dumped. I wasn't ready to get serious, and they started wanting more than I was willing to give. I can't think of anyone down there who'd be willing to take me to the party, when it would be a one-time thing. I'm coming back here the next day."

"And you haven't met anyone here?" Brittany asked. "I don't suppose any of the guys who work for your uncle would do?"

Eleanor covered her face with her hands. "That sounds so bad. I'm not a snob, really! Most of the guys who work for him are married or older. I haven't met any young, single guys there, and even if there was one, it would be awkward."

"What about church? You go to Riverdale with your aunt and uncle, don't you?"

"Well, I will when I have time. So far, I've been busy or just want to relax and sleep in after working all week. I plan to get there soon, though."

"I don't know if there are a lot of single guys there, though," Brittany said. "You could try a church in St. Cloud."

That made Eleanor laugh. "Go to church in St. Cloud in hopes of meeting a man? I'm not that desperate."

Brittany settled herself more comfortably on the stool, considering the question. "You could go out to a nightclub. That's what single people do, right?"

"Not me," Eleanor said. "Do you?"

"No, but I have a fiancé."

"Can I borrow him for Valentine's Day?" Her question was only half in jest.

"No!" Brittany slapped at Eleanor's hand. "You cannot. Oh! What about a dating website?" Brittany picked up her phone and tapped on the screen. "There are Christian ones. You might find someone there."

"He doesn't have to be a Christian," Eleanor said, "as long as he's not something weird."

"I just meant that it might be safer. Guys who sign up there will be expecting a girl with some moral standards. They're not just looking for a hook-up.

"Oh, right. Still... I don't think that sounds very safe, and if my parents found out, they'd kill me." Eleanor stood up. "I'd better get back to work. Thanks for listening to me whine, and thanks for the coffee break. It was good to get out of the office and have a little female companionship for a change."

5

David looked over the top of his laptop screen and contemplated his feet, propped on the coffee table. His mom's handknit socks never quite matched each other, but they were warm. Would his wife knit socks? She might, or maybe she would be more interested in fishing or hiking. Or playing the violin or driving a race car. Or flirting with other men and shopping for things he couldn't afford. You couldn't order up a wife like a sandwich on a menu.

His gaze returned to the computer. He'd read every page of the website at least twice. It looked decent, and there was a free trial. It wasn't specifically Christian, though—just founded on "Christian principles." Still, the goal was traditional marriage, and he was pretty traditional. He clicked on the privacy tab and scanned the fine print again. They promised to destroy his information if he requested it.

What if it was a train wreck? What if it was a success? What if people found out about it, either way? Would it damage his chances of entering the ministry if a church knew he'd found his wife online? David closed the computer and shifted it from his lap to the couch next to him.

"O, Lord. I'm not hearing Your voice here. I don't

want to do anything outside of Your will." David fell silent and waited. Nothing. Was he overthinking it? There was no commitment—no harm in just filling out the application and seeing what they said.

He set the computer on the coffee table and opened it. The website opened with a tap of the mouse. Betwixt Two Hearts. Silly name, but it was better than Virtual Dreams Digital Dating. He'd backed out of that one right away and been afraid to google for more options. Betwixt Two Hearts would have to do.

David scooted forward and hunched over the computer. He flexed his fingers and began to fill in blanks.

The coffee house had been transformed overnight, from Christmas to Valentine's Day, nearly six weeks ahead of time. David carried his coffee to a small table in the corner and checked his email for the third time since entering the building. Nothing from the matchmaking agency, of course. He'd only filled out the form last night. It would probably take a while, even if there were any girls in the area. He winced. What if there were a lot of college students on their list?

"Hey there. What's that look for?" Larry pulled out the chair and sat.

"Just borrowing trouble from tomorrow. I filled out a profile on that website you showed me, and now I'm getting cold feet."

"That's great—that you filled it out, I mean. I hope it works out. You never know about those places."

"Now you're skeptical? You were all for it two days

ago." Indignant, David dropped his phone on the table. "It just occurred to me that the only available women in this area might be college kids."

"Oh, yeah, that could be," Larry said. "I hope your new social life doesn't interfere with our lunches."

"Work and school are starting to interfere with our lunches," David admitted. "I only have half an hour today. We had our monthly meeting this morning, and it ran late. I don't know how we can spend two hours discussing stuff and not have anything significant to say or change."

"Those things are just to keep in touch. Employee bonding or something like that. There's my number." Larry shoved his chair backward, jostling the table behind him.

The blonde girl seated there grabbed her computer before it could slide off the table, but the mouse escaped, hitting the floor and tumbling under Larry's feet. He stepped on it and staggered like a slap stick comedian, clutching at their own table. David prudently lifted the coffee cups.

"Oh, man, I'm sorry." The big man picked up the remains of the mouse. "I think it's dead."

She regarded the bits and pieces. "Yes, it looks dead."

"Let me pay for it." Larry put the mouse on the table and pulled out his wallet. "I don't have any cash." He turned to David. "Do you have any cash?"

David shook his head. "Sorry, I don't." He looked around. "No cash machine in here, but you could probably go buy something and get cash back."

"No," said the girl. "Don't bother. I can afford a new mouse."

"No, I broke it; I'll pay for it." Larry stomped off,

calling over his shoulder. "Hang on. Don't leave."

The girl stared after him, clearly exasperated, before standing to put the tables and chairs back in order. David jumped up to help. "Sorry about that."

"I don't know why they put these tables so close together."

"They can squeeze more people in this way," David said. He sought words to fill the awkward wait. "Sorry about your mouse."

"Not your fault. I think I'm the only person who still uses one. I just can't seem to get the knack of using the pad."

Her eyes were denim blue. Not sky blue, or like sapphires or forget-me-nots, but like denim. Like his favorite jeans or the jacket his dad wore on his motorcycle. David had never seen eyes quite that color.

The eyes disappeared as she dropped her gaze to the table, and he realized he'd been staring, not listening to her words.

"Um, I use one, too. I'm an engineer, and the mouse works better for drafting."

She nodded, not meeting his eyes. She probably thought he was a creep. David dropped into his chair. No wonder he had to use an online dating service. No social skills at all.

"Here you go." Larry reappeared and dropped money on the girl's table. "I am really sorry."

"It didn't cost that much." She picked up one of the bills and handed the rest back to him. "Please. Thank you for covering it."

Larry wavered briefly before putting the bill in his pocket. "Sorry." Reseated, with his back to the girl, he grimaced at David, obviously aware of the girl's proximity and finding it difficult to resume normal conversation. "So, how'd your prayers come out? Any better than last time?"

"No, not really. I had some questions, and I haven't got a response yet." Behind his friend, he saw the blond girl lift her head from the computer screen, blue eyes wide and surprised.

Before he could think of a way to rephrase his answer, Larry went on.

"Why is it taking so long?" He forked a bite of salad into his mouth and continued talking around it. "Oh, right. You said he was getting married. Maybe he's been busy with his new bride."

The absurdity of the conversation and the girl's fascinated expression—she wasn't even pretending not to listen—suddenly struck David as hilarious. He burst into laughter, immediately regretful when she snatched up her computer and stalked away. She left the broken mouse on the table.

"What?" Larry raised his brows.

It wasn't worth explaining. "It's harder than you'd think to write out prayers."

"I didn't think there was a right or wrong way to pray."

"There's not, really," David said, "but Professor Neresen says we should understand all the elements if we're going to be able to help other people learn to pray."

"That's what I mean. You're saying there's a certain way they have to learn."

David rubbed his chin. "But what would you say if someone asked you how to pray?"

"I'd tell them you just talk to God like you would a person."

"That's right, but there's more to it, too. Adoration,

confession, thanksgiving, supplication... those are just words we made up to remind us, but he says we shouldn't ignore them, because Scripture says to do them. Praise God, confess your sins, give thanks, pray for the needs of others as well as our own. You don't do all of those things every time you pray, but you do need to be doing them. It sounds easy, but this is a really intense class."

Larry didn't look convinced. "If you say so. Hey, you're late. Sorry about the interruption." He cut his eyes to the side and gave a small backward jerk of his head.

"She's gone. She heard you say that God was busy with His new wife and took off." David chuckled.

It was the free trial that sucked her in. The respectable dating sites—if there was such a thing—were expensive. The cheaper ones—and especially the free ones—gave her the willies. According to one website, nearly 30% of single Americans were using online dating apps. That same website informed her that over half of their members lied on their profiles. Caveat emptor. Buyer beware.

Eleanor drummed her fingers on the keyboard as she read the Betwixt Two Hearts website: Christian principles, traditional marriage, not required to have a certain faith, treat others with respect, terminate account at any time. Perfect. She didn't want to get married, but otherwise it looked good. She clicked back to the registration page, grinning as she typed in her name with a flourish. Whatever would her mother say?

Ten minutes later, she leaned back in the leather recliner and considered the computer screen. She'd done the easy part; now she had to come up with creative answers, to attract the kind of man she needed. The matching was done by computer, unless you asked for a personal matchmaker. A computer would be better. She could game the system, work the algorithms...

She couldn't do it. Eleanor picked up her phone and tapped a text to Brittany.

WANT TO MEET FOR COFFEE TOMORROW? LUNCH? DINNER AFTER WORK?

The reply was immediate.

SURE. LUNCH WHERE WE HAD COFFEE? NOON?

That was easy. Explanations would have taken forever by text. Eleanor made a smiley emoticon and typed.

THANKS! SEE YOU THEN.

"Teachers are used to eating fast. And working while we eat." Eleanor pushed her plate aside and opened her laptop. "I tried to do it at home, and it was... I just need some ideas."

"Ideas?" Brittany peeled back the top of her cup and stirred her coffee with the little plastic stick. "Isn't it just a matter of answering the questions?"

"Yes, but they aren't true/false or multiple choice. I have to come up with answers that get me matched up with the right kind of guy."

"I hadn't thought of that," Brittany said. "It's not

like you're going down a list and picking the guy you like best. You have to fit their criteria, too."

"Right. A computer will match me up with a man like myself—similar interests, for example—so I need to list the right kind of interests."

"Huh." Brittany stood up and dragged her chair around so she could see the computer screen. "Nice profile pic. You look professional, which seems appropriate, because this looks a lot like a job application. You said you're a teacher?"

"Yes, I think that'll work better than 'take-off technician.'" Eleanor chuckled. "I'm not sure I'm even qualified to be called that, but I am qualified to teach. More than qualified. And Evergreen Services sounds like it might be some kind of educational service provider, right?" She clicked and scrolled. "Some of these questions are so open-ended! What is the most important thing you are looking for in another person? What do you notice first when meeting someone? I don't know!"

"Like you said, it's not true/false. Just put something generic in there. Kindness, a sense of humor, and honesty are important."

"Oh, and reliability. I like that in a person." Eleanor entered the response. "So, for the first thing I notice?"

"Eyes, smile, laugh."

"Okay, and then this one." Eleanor pointed at the screen. "What are you looking for in a relationship? So far, I have 'an honest, sensible man with a stable job, between the ages of 27 and 39.' Can you think of anything else I should add?"

She looked up hopefully and found the other girl staring at her.

"Eleanor, you sound like you're ordering something

from a menu. A medium-well burger with ketchup and pickle on a whole wheat bun with a side of fries."

Eleanor frowned. "Don't you think it's best to be straightforward when you want something specific?"

"Maybe, but not for this. You're looking for a relationship, not a hamburger."

"I'm looking for a date," Eleanor corrected. "I tried to think of someone in the Cities or here. The only people I know are my cousins, and I can't ask them to take me." She kicked the table leg. "Laurie keeps texting and calling me and sending me links. This thing sounds more like a wedding than an anniversary party. It's bigger every time I talk to her, and she wants to tell me every single detail. And the way she talks... it's almost like she knows I don't have a date and is trying to make me admit it."

"Would that be so bad?" Brittany asked.

"Yes. And this part—what do you think? I said I prefer a Protestant Christian. My parents don't have a problem with other religions, but it would be easier if he's Lutheran or Methodist or something."

"How about you? Do you have a preference?"

Eleanor shrugged. "Well, if I was really looking for a husband, he'd have to be a Christian, of course, as long as he was in a normal denomination. I was here yesterday, and there were these really strange guys at the next table. They said God was married. I moved away so I wouldn't get hit by lightning."

"Seriously? God got married?" Brittany asked. "Wow."

"They sounded serious. But then one of them laughed, so I didn't know if they were just playing a joke on me or what."

Brittany leaned forward. "Are you a Christian?"

"Yes, of course. I was practically raised in the church. I was baptized and did confirmation and the whole thing. I haven't been in a while, but you don't have to go to church to have a relationship with God." She hoped she didn't sound as defensive as she felt. Religion was on the list of things her mother said shouldn't be discussed in polite conversation, along with politics and something else. Probably money.

"Well, no, but..." Brittany looked troubled. "It's easier if you do, and you might meet some nice people there."

"You said there weren't any. I'm going to give this a shot. What do you think about divorced men?"

"I don't know. I'd have to know more about him. But if you're just looking for a date, it probably doesn't matter."

Was that sarcasm in her friend's voice? She didn't want to offend Brittany. She was the only person she'd met here, outside of her family, and they were all busy with their own lives.

"I'm not opposed to pursuing a relationship if we like each other. I guess I've been so focused on this stupid party that I can't think that far ahead. I've got to get through this." Eleanor rubbed her temple. "Anyhow, I said I'd prefer no kids."

"Don't you like kids?"

"Yeah, but they'd probably get sick on Valentine's Day, just when I need him."

At the other girl's expression, she said, "I know... I know. I need to get this out of the way first. You should have been there, at Christmastime. Laurie was working on seating charts. She seems to think I'd feel left out if she didn't share all the planning with me."

"Because you're the daughter and she's just the daughter-in-law?" Brittany suggested.

"Maybe. I hadn't thought of that. I'm perfectly happy to have her do it. It wouldn't even have occurred to me to have a party. I'm a failure as a Nielson daughter, so I'm glad she's there. She can keep my mother distracted with parties and grandchildren."

"I'm sure you're not a failure. You're just different, and it may take them a while to realize that."

Eleanor shook her head and pointed at the screen. "This is what I wrote for my interests: Reading, music, theater, art museums, classical music concerts, and travel."

"Seriously?" Brittany whooped with laughter. "How's that working out for you here? The high school has a band and drama club, but otherwise we're a little lacking in those things."

"Well, I'm not limiting them to this area. I said to search within a 50-mile radius. That will include the cities, too. Here." She turned the computer toward her friend. "Can you just proofread it for me, please? I really don't want to turn it in with typos!"

If it was all computer-generated, it shouldn't be taking so long. Eleanor refreshed her email page twice before closing the laptop. She wiggled her feet into her slippers and stood up, stretching, stiff after a day spent nestled in the overstuffed leather sofa. It had been a beautiful day, spent reading and watching the snow fall in big globby puffs. If all her winter days at the cabin were just like this one, she'd stay forever. She hadn't felt so peaceful in... ever.

The familiar scraping of a snowplow broke the quiet of the midafternoon dusk. Even better. Eleanor didn't really want to be snowed in. She opened the door, and a knee-high drift of snow fell on her feet. How had so much snow accumulated so quickly and quietly? Gary waved as he pushed a swath across the front—the back—of the house. Eleanor waved back, smiling. He was a good guy. She grabbed the stiff broom and swept the steps and walkway. The snow was heavier than she had expected, though, and fuzzy slippers were not an adequate substitute for boots. Her teeth were chattering by the time she finished the short path to the garage. She hurried back inside, stomping snow from her slippers before pulling them off. Maybe Uncle Gary would like some coffee. She looked out the window in time to see his tail lights vanish into the distance. He wasn't even coming inside?

The happy feelings evaporated, leaving her cold, wet, and a little lonely. And it was dark already, before five o'clock, so she couldn't even see the beautiful snow. What if it started snowing again overnight, and she really was snowed in? Dejected, she dropped onto the couch and covered herself with the fleece throw before pulling the computer onto her lap.

Still no mail. Maybe this whole business was a scam. It could be identity theft; they had a lot of information about her now. She navigated to the website and clicked on her profile. Still pending. She clicked on the About page, hoping for reassurance. Nothing new. She googled Betwixt Two Hearts and found mentions of it on a few blogs, but it was too new to have any reviews. She clicked on her profile again and sat up straight, nearly knocking the computer off her lap. Match found.

"No!" Appalled, Eleanor gazed at the picture of David Reid. The man from the coffee shop. He was presentable, even good-looking, but could she trust him to carry on appropriate conversation? Her mother would drive to Milaca and pack up Eleanor's belongings herself if she thought her daughter was involved with a religious nut.

She continued reading. Mechanical engineer. He'd said he was an engineer. Eleanor wondered if he ever worked with Evergreen Services. She'd have to ask Uncle Gary. David was 30 years old, played the guitar, liked being outdoors and doing photography.

"A seminary student? What kind of seminary does he attend?" She curled her legs underneath her and tugged the throw closer. He'd seemed normal before that conversation she'd overheard. Aside from the religious angle, he might work out. She could hint him away from church talk.

He was exactly what she needed, otherwise. Her parents would probably approve of him. He had a respectable job and was continuing his education. She scrolled, and there it was... he coached basketball and worked with underprivileged kids. Her parents would love him. Laurie would probably plan a wedding, pleased that the matter of the nanny would be resolved.

6

And there it was. Despite his previous impatience, it suddenly struck David that the matchmaker couldn't have spent much time on it. He circled the email link with the cursor, reluctant to click, as if opening the email would be making a commitment. It was just a suggestion, right? The matchmaker had a girl for him to meet. That was all.

He clicked on the email and again on the link inside. Then he had to sign in. Each little step seemed to be a little closer to commitment. He paused—again—before clicking on the little heart. What about her? Was this woman—his match—expecting him to contact her immediately? Did she think of this as a direct path to marriage? What if she was all wrong? He didn't want to hurt her. What if he liked her and she rejected him?

"Stop it." He'd never thought of himself as insecure before, but this whole business was tying him up in knots. "Everyone's doing it. It's just a suggestion." His words didn't reassure him. Talking to himself was probably a bad sign, too.

He clicked on the heart and saw her picture. His breath caught in his throat. The girl with the denim eyes. The one whose mouse Larry had broken. The one who'd been so shocked at their conversation that she'd run away.

David groaned and leaned back against the couch cushions.

Under different circumstances, he'd be thrilled. She was gorgeous, with thick blond hair, blue eyes, a smooth complexion and rose-pink lips. Rose-pink? David shook his head in disbelief. Where did that come from? But none of that mattered. Last time he'd seen her, she'd been practically running away from him.

Eleanor Nielson, teacher. She looked elegant in her profile picture, but no prettier than she had in denim leggings and a long plaid shirt. Not that he'd noticed her clothing, of course. Not really. Was she a local teacher? She liked classical concerts, art museums, and reading. David frowned. None of those things had been on his list, unless you counted playing the guitar in the worship band at church.

She was a Christian. Maybe that's why they'd been matched. Or maybe there was no one else in the neighborhood. Why would a woman like her need to use a matchmaking service? And what was he supposed to do now? She must have received his profile, too, and recognized him. What was she thinking? Would she give him a chance, or would she email the company and tell them to try again? It would be rude to ignore her, though. He could email the company first, to see if they'd heard from her, or wait a day or so to see if they emailed him.

David stood up and stretched. He had to pull himself together. He wasn't a nervous adolescent anymore. He could handle a date with a woman. Or rejection. Whichever came first.

Almost there. David lengthened his stride to avoid the appearance of running, but Angela had no such scruples. The girl was fast, and she knew he wasn't really deaf.

"David!"

He stopped, hand on his car door, beaten but not defeated. "Hi, Angela. You just caught me. I'm on my way to the Y for basketball."

"You forgot this." She extended his phone.

"Oh, Thanks."

"You have a UMD bumper sticker. Is that where you went to college?"

"Yeah. School of Engineering."

"I went to Van Bramer."

Years of his mother's training prevented him from escaping into his car. "Um... is that around here?"

"No, in Connecticut."

Something was off. David shifted his weight from one foot to another, relieved when she broke the brief silence. "You've probably never heard of it."

"No, I haven't." If he'd ever thought about it—which he hadn't—he would have guessed community college, for a degree in cosmetology. She always looked nice. "What was your major?" It would be beyond rude to ask if she graduated.

"Most people go there to get their MRS. My degree was in applied data management."

Computers. Huh. "Well, I'd better get going. Thanks for the phone." He raised it in farewell.

She turned and walked away before he finished. Had he offended her? He hadn't meant to do that... he just wanted to get away. He was inside the car, starting the engine, before he realized the difference in their conversation. He'd never heard her talk about herself before. He knew practically nothing about her, except that she was Cal's sister and always hanging around the office.

He might not be a psychologist, like Larry, but even he knew she probably craved male attention because she was insecure. Their father died when she was a baby, and Cal wasn't exactly a nurturing big brother. David sighed. He should invite her to church. But Eleanor...

"I'm glad you came. You're really moving since you lost so much weight. There usually aren't so many guys here, and I was running late. I stopped by the office after church, and Angela caught me. I mean, I forgot my phone inside and she ran it out to me."

"I've only lost twenty pounds so far," Larry said. "How's Angela doing?"

"Fine. Have you ever heard of a Van Bramer College, in Connecticut?"

"I don't think so. Why?"

"Angela said she went there. She got a degree in applied data management. I assume it's a bachelor's degree, but she said they have an MRS program. Do you have any idea what that is?"

Larry gazed at him, head tipped to one side, until David had to break the silence.

"What?"

His friend reached around him and used a gloved finger to write "Mrs." on the back window of David's car. "Those credentials are usually listed before a woman's name instead of at the end of it."

David blinked. "Oh. Well, then. Angela didn't get that degree. She studied computers."

"You need to get out more," Larry said. "You engineers have a very limited knowledge of the world outside your workshop."

That stung. He was going to be a pastor. He needed to be in the world.

Larry continued. "Our receptionist has a degree in applied data management. She's a bit overqualified, but she's waiting for the administrative assistant to retire, so she can move into that position. A secretary. With another five or six years of experience, she'll be looking for a job as an administrative professional. Then she'll be running the place, but the world will still think of her as a secretary or bookkeeper."

"I wonder why Angela can't find a job, then. It seems like everyone's hiring right now."

Larry frowned. "She has a job. She works for Cal."

"Doing what? We have a woman who manages all that stuff."

"I dunno, but apparently she's pretty important. Meg says Angela's the real genius behind Ridgewell Mechanical Engineering."

David reluctantly quelled the smart-alecky comments that occurred to him. Too bad... there were some real zingers. Self-control, subdue the tongue. It wasn't the first time he'd jumped to conclusions based on incomplete evidence, in science and in human interactions. He changed the subject.

"Hey, I got a response from the Betwixt Two Hearts agency, and you won't believe who it is."

"Angela?"

"No! It's that girl from the coffee shop. The one whose mouse you broke."

Larry laughed. "Really? That's a coincidence. Have you talked to her yet?"

"Not yet," David said, "but she's seen my picture, and I'm sure she remembers us. Her name's Eleanor Nielson, and she's a teacher. She's from Milaca."

"That sounds promising. So now what? Do you exchange emails, or meet up, or what?"

"The website has a kind of messaging system. I'm hoping she'll initiate that, but I don't know. She got up and left, remember? You were talking about my professor being married, it sounded like you were talking about God. I think you scared her off."

"Sure, blame me. Let me know how it works out. Maybe I'll try it myself." Larry looked up at the heavy sky. "I think we're going to get more snow tonight."

"All day tomorrow, from the sounds of it. I went out skiing on Platke Lake yesterday, but it was a pretty wet snow. A few more inches and some colder weather will help."

"I hope to get back to skiing," Larry said as he tossed his duffel bag into his car, "but it won't be cross-country. That's more work than fun. Does your Eleanor ski?"

"I don't know. I hope so." But her profile hadn't listed outdoor activities. David hoped that was an oversight. He didn't have anything against classical music and art museums, but that kind of thing wasn't his first choice for how to spend his limited free time. "She likes music."

"Music is good. Does she know you play guitar?"

"I put it on my profile. I wrote that I play on the worship team at church."

"Speaking of worship," Larry said, "you've got the over-sixty crowd singing louder than I've ever heard before, with those old songs of yours. Where do you get that stuff?"

"The sixties, man." David pointed upward. "The great revival of the seventies. The Jesus People. That's where contemporary Christian music began."

"I hadn't realized it was that long ago."

"My grandparents were in it. Jesus People, Jesus Freaks... My mom says Grandma was a Keith Green groupie."

"I've heard of him," Larry said. "We spent a lot of time studying that whole time period in my last year of school. It wasn't just the Jesus People... there was the Back to the Land movement, the hippies with free love and communes, new secular music, drugs, student protests, Vietnam and all sorts of rebellion, set against the backdrop of space exploration, the invention of the computer, the assassinations of President Kennedy and Martin Luther King, civil rights, Watergate, Cuba, the Cold War." He shook his head. "That's what will keep me in business for a few more generations."

He'd never seen Larry so animated. "I hadn't really thought about it in that bigger context," David admitted. "Just the revivals and the Jesus music. I'm glad my grandparents went that direction instead of into LSD and free love, but I have a feeling my grandpa would have been one of the men in horn-rimmed glasses, building giant computers in bunkers rather than wearing bell bottoms and beads at Woodstock." The image made him chuckle and then laugh out loud. "I can't imagine that at all. Grandma, maybe, but not Grandpa."

"Paradox," Larry said with relish. "It was an age of

exploding ideas and change. Psychologists were the new super scientists, experimenting on prisoners and college students with exotic drugs and weird tests. MK-Ultra."

"Yeah, those were the days," David said. "Now, you just listen to girls complain about their wedding planning."

Eleanor pulled the phone away from her ear and stared at the screen in disbelief. Seriously? She tapped the speaker button and tossed the phone on the passenger seat.

Her sister-in-law continued, as placid as ever. "I wanted a cruise to Alaska, but Zack insists they'd rather go to St. John. It'll have to be in the summer, though, and who wants to go to the Caribbean in the summer? That's definitely a winter vacation."

"A cruise? For a thirty-fifth wedding anniversary?"

"No, that's what I'm saying." Was there the faintest hint of impatience in Laurie's voice? "Zack didn't want the cruise. We found a good deal at an all-inclusive place in St. John. And now Soren's mad because he was just getting them a weekend in Chicago, to see Wicked and that Japanese exhibit at the Art Institute."

"What's Robert getting them—a new car?" She regretted the sarcasm even as the words escaped. "I can't afford an expensive gift, Laurie."

"The biggest gift you could give your parents would be to come back -"

"Stop!" Eleanor shouted at the phone. "No, I'm not doing that. Not now, anyhow. I didn't know we were going to be giving them gifts at all."

"It would be strange to have a party in their honor

and not give them gifts. We wrote 'no gifts' on the invitations, of course, but that doesn't apply to us. But if you don't have a gift for them, they're not going to be upset. They'll just be glad to have you at the party."

Eleanor wished she could afford a new phone. She'd throw this one out the window, just for the satisfaction of watching it smash into a thousand pieces. She'd been home three times since leaving three months ago, including extended visits at Thanksgiving and Christmas.

"Okay, Laurie. I'll come up with something. I'm driving now. Talk to you later. Love you. Bye." She jabbed at the disconnect button on the last word. Would the party issue be better or worse if she lived there? Just different, she decided. Her parents would be happy, but she'd be coming home with headaches after school every day, wishing she'd chosen a different career. Anything. She'd make a good mechanical contractor, like Uncle Gary, if she didn't have to work in the field. She could have been an engineer, like David. No, she liked what she saw of Gary's job. He didn't just design things; he built them. He made them happen. Her mother would have a meltdown if she knew Eleanor liked the idea of going into construction.

Her amusement faded at the sight of her uncle. Gary sat with his back against the picnic table, his head down, leg extended, arms were wrapped around his midsection.

He looked up as she slammed the car door and ran toward him. "What are you doing here?"

"I work here." The idiotic response slipped out.

"It's going to snow again. You should have stayed home." He started to shake his head and groaned. "I fell, getting out of the truck. Slipped on the ice. I think I broke my ankle." He gave an unexpected snort. "Just like Aunt Violet. She'll love that."

"Did you call for help?"

"Phone's in the truck. I just needed to sit down for a minute."

"Wait here." She winced, glad she couldn't see his reaction to that as she hurried to her car. She tapped in 911 on her way back to him.

"Give me that." Gary reached for the phone, and his left arm fell to his lap. Moaning, he curled forward, cradling it against his body.

Eleanor conveyed all the information to the operator, ignoring her uncle's interruptions.

"The ambulance will be there in 15 minutes, ma'am. Can you stay on the phone?"

"No, I cannot. I need to get my uncle some blankets and something hot to drink." She was freezing, and Uncle Gary had been out longer than her, injured.

He looked terrible, all pink and white, shuddering with every breath, and he hadn't spoken in several minutes. Eleanor tried not to jar him as she tucked her emergency blanket around him. "I know it's not very warm, since it's been in the back of the car all winter, but it's all I have. I'll be right back. I'm going to get you some coffee. Is the office locked?"

He grunted. "Keys. Under truck."

Eleanor squatted, glad the truck's big tires lifted it higher than her SUV. She couldn't see the keys in the shadows; they must have skidded across the ice when Gary fell.

"Couldn't reach the phone. Couldn't reach the keys. I'm just going to rest my eyes until the ambulance gets here."

"No!" Eleanor grabbed the door handle as she rose, sliding on the ice. They'd be in trouble if both of them got hurt. "Don't go to sleep." What if he had a concussion? He could have internal injuries, too, and he was on his way to hypothermia.

She turned back to the truck and took a deep breath of icy air. "Okay, I can do this." She got down on her hands and knees and then scooted forward on her stomach, groping blindly for the keyring. It was here somewhere.

She jerked upward at the sound of a car engine, banging her head on the undercarriage. Her shriek was lost under the call of the new arrival.

"Hey! Are you okay?"

Too soon for the ambulance. Eleanor caught sight of the keyring and stretched. Her bare fingers, wet and cold, pushed the keys further away. She growled.

"She's under the truck. Ambulance coming."

Suddenly Uncle Gary could talk? A bubble of hysterical laughter rose in her. The man would think Gary had run her over. Eleanor wiggled sideways and hooked the edge of the ring.

"Can you hear me?"

The voice was uncomfortably close to her legs. So embarrassing. "I'm fine." Eleanor tried to scoot backward, but the man grasped her boot.

"Don't move. The ambulance is on the way."

"I'm fine! I'm freezing!"

"The ambulance will be here in just a few minutes. You shouldn't be moved until they get here, in case you have back or neck injuries."

"I don't!" Eleanor kicked free of his restraint. "I'm not hurt." She gasped as a drop of blood fell on the ice in front of her. She must have cut her head. A shudder of revulsion went through her at the flow of warmth on her forehead. She was bleeding, and she was freezing. "Pull me out!"

"But..."

"Now! Pull me out!"

The stranger complied. He squatted in front of her, a silhouette against the white sky, as she rolled to a sitting position. She pushed her hair off her face and jumped up, horrified at the blood.

"Sit down! I thought you said you weren't injured!"

"I'm not. I was just getting the keys." Still clutching the ring, she wiped her hands on her wet jeans and turned toward the office. Out of the corner of her eye, she saw blood in her hair. Her head hurt. Her legs trembled.

"Wait." The man reached for her and she stepped away from him.

"I can't wait. I need to go inside and make some coffee." Her voice rose on the last three words. She really was hysterical now.

"You're bleeding." The man grasped her arm. "And... you're Eleanor Nielson."

"Uncle Gary needs something hot to drink!"

Even as she yelled at him—actually yelled—she was conscious of a new horror. She drew herself up as tall as possible, composed, in control. Calm. Authoritative. "No, I'm not."

His mouth curved in a smile. "Yes, you are. I have coffee in my car—a latte, with milk and sugar. Come on." He took her elbow and led her to the table. "I'll get the coffee."

7

See, now, you'll be much more comfortable here." Violet's voice was smug.

She'd have no privacy, and she'd be spending all her time with her elderly aunt, who seemed to have plenty of jobs lined up for the two of them to do together. Eleanor missed the cabin already.

She dropped onto the bed and smiled at Violet. "It's good of you to have me. I hope I can be helpful." White lies and good manners. "I know you've been looking forward to living alone, so I'll stay out of your way as much as possible. Let me know what I can do to help out with cooking and cleaning—or whatever you need. I'm sure I'll have enough money saved by spring to get into a place of my own."

"There's no hurry. Like I told you last time, I have some projects I need help with. You'll be doing me a favor."

"Great." Eleanor looked around the bedroom. "I'll just get my clothes unpacked, and we can make some plans."

Aunt Violet sat down in the rocking chair. "I can talk while you work. I can even talk while I work, if you need a hand with that."

"No, thanks, I can do it. I don't have much with me."

Resigned, she unzipped the smallest suitcase and opened the top dresser drawer. Lilac-printed paper lined the drawer, an unexpected and old-fashioned touch in this modernized house. "That's pretty! And what a nice dresser. Is it a family heirloom?"

Her aunt nodded. "It was mine, but I have a new one I like better. Your mother used this one, I think, right here in this very room. Maria put that paper in it for her, because she loved lilacs."

Eleanor paused. "My mother? This was her room?"

"She shared it with Colleen, but the dresser was hers. Does she still like lilacs?"

"I think so. We have some in the backyard. She used to cut branches and bring them inside."

Violet pointed through the window. "See those over there? She made your uncle Olof plant those. Kristina said apple trees would be more practical, but Kathy wanted lilacs, and she had Olof wrapped around her little finger. He got a dozen suckers from the neighbor and planted them right under Kristina's nose." Violet chuckled. "It was just about the only time anyone ever stood up to Kristina. Anyhow, your mom watered them every day all summer, even if it had rained overnight. Olof fertilized them when he did the garden. Oh, they adored each other."

Eleanor tried to imagine her mother as a little girl, hand-in-hand with a doting uncle. Impossible. Mom seldom talked about her family at all. She walked to the window. "Those are lilacs? They look more like trees."

"They still bloom pretty good in the spring, but they could probably use some pruning." Violet said. "Maybe she'll come out and see them. That would be nice. She'd probably enjoy seeing the annex, too. It was always a nice place, not old like the rest of the farmhouse, but it's even better now that Carl fixed it up for me."

Aunt Violet missed her—a young niece she'd known since infancy. Why hadn't Mom been out to see her? She should have been. Eleanor would invite her—would insist.

"I had the impression she was really little when they moved into town. A preschooler."

"No, she was nine or ten, I think." Violet shook her head. "Colleen was a chatterbox, but Kathy was quiet. She liked reading and being outside by herself or with Olof. The farm was better for her than town. I'm afraid she was teased in school and didn't have a lot of friends."

Interesting. "She said she had a good teacher here, who inspired her to become a teacher herself."

"Oh, yes," Violet said. "Maybel Furster. She was a fine woman."

"She died recently, didn't she?" asked Eleanor. "Mom was upset."

"She did. Cancer. It was sad, but a beautiful Home-going. She'd picked out all her favorite songs. 'Lots of singing,' she said. We nearly took the roof right off the building with In Christ Alone."

Eleanor blinked. A beautiful Home-going? She'd never heard that expression. It must mean going to heaven. Going home?

"She never had a husband or children, you know," Violet continued. "She just poured herself into her students at school and the Sunday school students at church. She had hundreds of people at her funeral, and only good words spoken or thought of her."

"That's lovely." A lump blocked Eleanor's throat. Was that why her mother felt so strongly about teaching, with a role model like that? How wonderful it would be, to have such an impact and reputation. "Did my mother have her as a Sunday school teacher, too?"

"Most likely. We all went to that church until they moved to town. My grandfather helped build it. That's what they did back then. They moved to America, built Lutheran churches and farmed. That church burned down about thirty years ago, and there weren't enough young people to rebuild it, so the rest of us either moved to the Methodist church or the new Riverdale one."

"Your grandfather! That would be my..." Eleanor ticked off the generations on her fingers. "Great, great, great grandfather?"

"Your second great-grandfather. I can show you on the family tree."

"I'd like that." At least, she might. Something about the gleam in Aunt Violet's eyes made her wary. "That's sad about the church, to split up after all those years together."

"There weren't many of us left. We still see each other."

Eleanor returned to her unpacking, eying Violet. The old woman had seen so much of this community, for so many years. More than almost anyone else in the area.

"Is it hard to adjust to all the changes?"

Her aunt shrugged. "Most of the time, change doesn't just happen all at once. It's gradual, and you don't realize it's changing until you look around and realize everything's different. She looked out the window. "Change is normal. It's usually fine, but sometimes it's bad—or just sad."

Eleanor sat on the bed, ignoring the suitcase full of clothing. "What do you mean?"

Violet twisted her fingers together in her lap before looking up at Eleanor. "When Maybel died, that was sad, but it wasn't bad. And it wasn't even a change. She was 95 years old and ready to move on. It's not bad at all, and just sad for us. She's doing fine."

"But some things are bad and sad, like when your church burned down. And wars."

"True enough." Violet rocked forward and pushed against the arms of the chair to stand up. "Change just happens, Nellie. Life moves on, never stopping, and we change with it. In the end, we go Home to the only eternal and unchanging God. That's really all that matters, in the end."

Eleanor watched her leave, wondering if she'd said something wrong. Their casual conversation had taken an odd turn. She pulled the plastic bag off the pile of clothes on hangers and started filling the closet. She'd not had opportunity to wear any of her good work clothes. Maybe she should just pack them away with everything else she had in storage. More things in storage, waiting for Eleanor to make up her mind. Would she discard them, use them, or leave them in storage—in limbo?

She walked to the window and tried again to picture her mother as a little girl, determined to have lilacs of her own. Stubborn and determined. Yes, that fit. And it fit her, too. If she wasn't stubborn and determined, she wouldn't be here now.

What was she going to do? Uncle Gary needed her, as many hours as she could work while he was in the rehab center, but when summer came, they'd be pressing her to come back for the start of the new school year. They truly believed that would be the best thing for her. They thought it would make her happy, because it made them happy.

But she wasn't like them. She didn't share their interests – their priorities. Teaching was a noble calling.

Shaping young minds, inspiring them to learn and grow, being someone like Maybel Furston. Why didn't it make her feel fulfilled?

No, she thought. It wasn't even a matter of fulfillment. She just didn't like doing it. And that made her feel terrible. What kind of monster didn't like helping children?

Her parents would be horrified and convinced she needed a counselor. Or an exorcist.

Still tall and erect, even in his wheelchair, Uncle Olof reached out to take her hand. "Hello." He had a full head of thick white hair, and unruly eyebrows over blue-gray eyes that matched his chambray shirt. They were like hers, Eleanor realized. A little lighter, maybe, but similar.

"This is Nellie, Olof. You've never met before, but she is Kathy's daughter. One of Soren's granddaughters."

His tentative, pleasant expression grew into a broad smile. "Nice to meet you, Nellie."

"It's nice to meet you. I'm sorry we interrupted the football game."

"Vikings were losing. No point in watching that happen again." He turned to Violet. "That nurse, the one with long hair, she says Gary's coming here. He's too young."

"Oh, it's just for a few weeks, for rehab." Violet said. "He slipped on the ice getting out of his truck. Somehow, he managed to dislocate his shoulder and also break the shoulder bone. His ankle's pretty bad, all broken up inside. They did one surgery already, and he'll need at least one more." She sat down on one of the wing chairs. "He has to come here because of his hip. He fell on it pretty hard and did something to the joint. It's not broken, but he can't walk on it yet. It might need surgery too. Oh, and he has a concussion and was in the early stages of hypothermia when the ambulance got there."

"He fell on the ice and did all that? He must have looked like Dick Van Dyke, with all those falls he used to do, on TV."

Eleanor grinned. It probably had looked a bit like that. The aftermath hadn't been so comical. "We're going over there to see him in a little bit. I work for him, you know, and he's making a list of everything I need to do while he's gone."

"Make him give you a raise," Olof said.

"Good idea." Eleanor sank onto the chair in front of him. "Aunt Violet's been telling me about you. She showed me the lilac bushes you planted with my mother, Kathy. They're so big now, like regular trees."

"Lilacs?" He looked at Violet. "What lilacs?"

"The lilacs you planted with Kathy, Olof. Do you remember those? It was a long time ago."

"Oh, a long time ago." He looked relieved. "I don't remember that."

"I'm looking forward to seeing them in bloom." Eleanor broke off when Violet shook her head.

"Lilacs." Olof nodded slowly. "A row of lilacs, right where Kristina wanted apple trees. Do you know..." He bent forward and lowered his voice. "I had to replant those things. She ran the mower over them. Accidentally, she said. Ha. Don't tell Kathy, though."

"Okay." Eleanor looked to Violet for guidance.

"No, of course not." Violet stood, pulling on her

gloves. "How was your dinner tonight, Olof? Meatloaf, right? Was it any better than last time? I told them you didn't want the onions in it."

He nodded. "It was better. Thanks for coming by." He looked at Eleanor. "Thanks for coming."

"It was nice to meet you. I'm sure I'll be back."

"Good, good." He wheeled himself to the door, waving as they left.

"I made him confused." Eleanor glanced back to where he was still sitting, watching them through the glass doors He waved. She waved back.

"He gets confused. He had a good spell before that, though. He knew who Gary was, and even Dick Van Dyke." Violet sounded pleased.

"He's still waving." Eleanor waved back. "Is he sad that we're leaving?"

"Maybe. Are you buckled up?"

"Yes." Eleanor gave a final wave and saw him wheel the chair away as Violet turned the car onto the street. "Does he get many visitors?"

"I get here nearly every day, but it's going to be harder now that I'm not in town anymore. Carl and Constance go, and they usually bring little Sarah. She plays checkers with him. Gary's there at least once a week, and your uncle Scott and his wife come when they can. They're up in Bemidji, and she's not in good health." She sighed. "It's hard."

"Well, Uncle Gary will be there every day, now! That will make Uncle Olof happy, won't it?"

"On his good days, yes. They can watch football games. They're all reruns, but Olof doesn't care. A game is a game. Baseball in the summer and football in the winter."

"What about his bad days?" Eleanor asked.

"Well, your uncle Gary will probably stay out of his way on those days, or just pretend to be a stranger."

"Pretend to be a stranger?" Shocked, Eleanor stared at Violet. "You mean, just act like they've never met? Wouldn't it be better to help Olof remember? Give him reference points, like you did today, when you said I was Kathy's daughter and one of Soren's granddaughters."

"He was having a good day today," Violet said, "and I started by telling him you'd never met before, so he wasn't afraid that he should already know you. We used to try to make him remember things. He'd be all worried about getting home, and we'd remind him that he lives here now, or he'd say he had to go help Papa in the barn, and we'd remind him that Papa passed away forty years ago."

She stopped at a traffic light and fell silent. Eleanor waited, hoping she'd continue. What would it be like, to be responsible for Soren or Robert or Zack in that situation?

"We tried. Then one day, a little girl—a CNA who couldn't have been more than five feet tall—came up and tugged on my elbow. I followed her into the hallway and got a lecture on how to treat people with Alzheimer's. She even printed up a list of guidelines for me."

Someone dared to lecture Aunt Violet? Eleanor hid a grin. "What did it say?"

"First of all, you don't insist they're wrong. They're anxious and afraid all the time, and it only distresses them when you confuse them more. If they do get upset, you distract them."

"Like you did when you asked about the meatloaf!" Eleanor said. "It seemed to work."

"If I hadn't distracted him, he would have worked himself up about the lilacs. And the biggest thing is that you don't tell them people are dead," Violet snapped. "How would you feel if you were upset and worried about your father, fully convinced he was looking for you, and someone kept insisting he was dead?"

"Oh. Yeah. But... it seems kind of like lying."

"So, lie," Violet said wearily. "Olof isn't going to get better. He doesn't need to be corrected. He needs to be loved and taken care of. I would have done it at home if I could, but he kept wandering off or doing dangerous things at home. This is a good place, and he's fine."

The argument, too distant for the words to be discernible, was obviously heated. Was that Uncle Gary? Easy-going, kind Uncle Gary? Eleanor cast a glance at Violet. The older woman rolled her eyes.

"Oh, for goodness sake. Men are such babies when they're sick."

But Uncle Gary wasn't sick. Eleanor followed the voices, walking faster than her aunt, and reached the room in time to hear the sweet coaxing voice, full of laughter, say "Oh, yes, you are. Come on, I'll give you another gown to cover your backside. You know how it is when you fall and break your hip. You have to get up and walk again, right away."

"It's not broken." He broke off at the sight of Eleanor. "If I'd known she was here, I'd have gone to a different hospital."

"Oh, Cheryl!" Aunt Violet pushed past Eleanor to embrace the therapist, who hugged her more tightly than seemed advisable with a frail, elderly woman. Violet didn't seem to mind. She drew back and patted the woman's cheek. "It's so good to see you again."

"You always did take her side," Gary muttered.

"Oh, stop." Cheryl held out her hand—to hold, not shake. "You must be Eleanor. I know your mom—knew her when she lived here, anyhow. How is she?"

"She's good." Did everyone here know her mother? This woman must be the same age, but she seemed more youthful, with a mop of blond, corkscrew curls and sparkling blue eyes.

"I'm Cheryl Anderson." She ignored the patient's rude snort. "Not a blood relative, but one in spirit."

"Not in law."

Gary must be in pain. Eleanor moved closer to the bed. "How are you?"

"I was better twenty minutes ago. I've been making a list for you, but she took it away."

"Therapy is on a tight schedule," Cheryl said, "and we've already wasted a lot of time." She held out a hand to Gary. He took it, and she helped him sit up and turn to the side of the bed. He used his free hand to pull the blanket across his lap.

"What about my ankle? I can't walk on that."

"Oh, I have a cart for that. It's just like a scooter. Do you ladies want to come with us?" She beamed at them, and Eleanor got it.

"Are you..."

"Your aunt!" Cheryl said triumphantly.

Gary moaned. "Ex-aunt."

"Oh, Gary." Cheryl sank onto the bed next to him. "I'm teasing you. I have a wheelchair in the hall. We're going down to the therapy room to do some measurements, and then they want to do an MRI on that hip. It'll take about an hour, all together."

"We can wait." Eleanor looked at Violet. "Is that okay?"

"Oh, yes. We can wait."

"I hope you can work a lot of overtime, Ellie." Gary rubbed his hand over his face. "I'm glad you're here. I'm going to need you."

He needed her. The words felt like a gift. An accolade. Eleanor nodded, hoping her face wasn't all scrunched up. "I'll be here."

She followed Violet into the hall, feeling better than she had in years. She wouldn't let him down.

"I can't believe she's here." Violet sounded exceptionally happy, too. "I always liked her. She was good for him. Stupid boy."

"Gary was a stupid boy?"

"They were too young to be married. I'm glad she's back." Violet stopped. "You know, I should visit my friend Josie while I'm here. Can you occupy yourself for an hour?"

"Yes, of course. I can meet you in Gary's room at..." Eleanor consulted her phone. "Ten o'clock."

"All right. I wonder if Josie knows that Cheryl's back."

8

Of course, his motives were mixed—no use pretending otherwise. Eleanor Nielson, after her determination to save her uncle, didn't seem like the kind of person to neglect him in the hospital. She might be here. Still, her sudden appearance, framed by the elevator doors and looking much happier than she had last time he'd seen her, rocked him back.

"Hi there!"

She blinked—in confusion? —and then smiled.

David blinked back, stunned. He'd seen her professional headshot, and he'd seen her soaking wet and blood-streaked, and even for those few minutes in the coffee shop, but he'd never seen that smile. He should have worn sunglasses.

"Hello! We meet again—and again, even without the help of that agency. If I didn't get the free trial, I'd ask for a refund."

"A refund?" It took him a minute to understand her statement. "True. It's been more providential than professional. We haven't corresponded through the agency at all."

"Right, and we don't need to do that now, do we?"

"No," he said. He tipped his head toward the elevator. "I was on my way to see Gary. How's he doing?"

"He's a mess, and his therapist is his ex-wife, who seems awfully cheerful to have him at her mercy." She clapped her hand over her mouth, her beautiful denim eyes widening. "Forget I said that. I guess I'm just so relieved to see him... that wasn't very discreet. Anyhow, he's gone for therapy and an MRI and won't be back for an hour."

"That must be an interesting situation. So, are you free until then?" David hoped she'd say yes. It would be so much easier than making a formal date, with time to work himself up into a nervous wreck.

She nodded slowly. "Yes, I am. We could get some coffee in the cafeteria."

"Perfect." Better than perfect. His lingering reservations vanished as they walked together. "I'm glad to see you again, without my good but clumsy friend. That was an awkward way to meet."

"It was," she said, "and the next one wasn't much better, with me a bloody mess, screaming at you. I can't imagine how you recognized me."

"I'd know you anywhere." Woah... way too fast. "I'd seen you at the coffee shop, too, not just the picture from the agency."

"I don't know... I looked pretty scary. The paramedics insisted I come in the ambulance."

He'd stayed until they left. She'd been too stressed to notice. "I'm glad you're okay. No concussion?"

"Just a typical scalp wound." She shivered. "And cold. That was the worst part. I was so cold, and shaking so hard, and all I could think about was how much worse it must be for Uncle Gary. I didn't know how long he'd been out there. He still doesn't remember anything after he fell, like how he made it to the bench."

"Probably just as well. It must have been painful."

He watched her as she ordered and paid for her coffee. Why would a girl like this need to use a matchmaking agency?

"Have you ever done this before? Online dating, I mean." She sat, sipping her coffee and wrinkled her nose. "This is awful."

"No, have you?"

"I haven't. A friend talked me into it. I mean, she showed me the website and encouraged me to fill it out, because she knew I... I was having trouble meeting people here. Brittany's the only person I know, outside my family. Even at work, I only ever see Uncle Gary."

David set his cup on the table. "You work for your uncle?"

"Yes. I'll be putting in a lot of overtime while he's in the hospital."

"But you said you were a teacher."

Eleanor wrapped her hands around her coffee cup and looked into the murky brew. Had she lied? Why?

"I am a teacher. I mean, I'm a certified teacher. I'm just taking a break to work for my uncle while I decide what I want to do with the rest of my life. While I find myself."

The air quotes and her droll tone might have been meant to hint him away from the topic, but he had to know more.

"You don't want to teach?"

"I don't know. I don't think so. At least, not right now. How about you? Your profile said you're in seminary. You're an engineer, but you want to be a minister?"

"Yes, eventually. It's an online master's program, with a few retreats and other hands-on activities."

"Is it for a particular denomination? I... uh... heard a bit of your conversation with your friend the other day."

"The part about God being married?" He grinned. "I got the impression we'd shocked you."

"Maybe I needed some context," Eleanor said. "I assume you were just joking."

"Not joking, but we were talking about my professor, not God. I think I said I'd sent some questions and not had an answer, and then Larry said it was taking a long time because the professor had just got married."

"Oh, that makes sense!" She looked relieved. "That will teach me to eavesdrop, right? I was afraid you might be a member of some strange cult."

"Nope, just a good, old-fashioned, Bible-believing, fundamental Christian. Fundamental with a lower-case f, I mean."

"Got it. So, is it a Lutheran or Methodist seminary?"

He shook his head. "Just a Bible school without affiliation with any major denomination. Protestant, of course. More reformed than not, but not Calvinist."

"But not some cult where God is married and too busy to answer prayers." She smiled, more mischievous than dazzling this time.

"No, it's pretty basic. How about you? Your profile said you live in Milaca. Do you go to church there, or here in St. Cloud?"

"My family goes to Riverdale in Milaca, and I go with them." She took another sip of coffee and set the cup on the table. "I haven't made it to church as often as I should. I've only been here a few months, and I was living out at my uncle's cabin on Tasker Lake until yesterday. I went back to the cities to spend Thanksgiving and Christmas with my parents."

"Minneapolis?" He tried to remember... had the profile covered that, or did it just list the current residence? "I thought you said your family was here."

"I grew up in Minneapolis. My parents and three brothers still live there—and a sister-in-law and a nephew and niece, too, and my dad's parents and siblings." She rolled her eyes. "A crowd. My mom grew up in Milaca, and some of her family is still here. Now that Uncle Gary's in the hospital, I've moved into the annex of the old family farmhouse, with my cousin and great-aunt.

"You didn't like the cabin?"

She picked up a stir stick and whirled it through her nearly-empty cup. "I couldn't live at the cabin without someone to plow, and... well, it was pretty isolated."

"Did it have indoor toilets and running water?"

Eleanor laughed. "It's definitely not a primitive cabin. It's one of those big prow-front places with a massive stone fireplace and enormous logs. It has everything, even internet and cable TV. Jet skis, a nice boat, snowmobiles... he has all the toys."

"It sounds great." He needed an uncle like that. His uncles had the cabins without indoor plumbing. "But you got lonely out there?"

She responded pensively. "It wasn't so much the loneliness as the emptiness. It was so vast, and the whole front of it's glass. I'm sure it's better in the summer, when days are longer. I worked all day, and it was dark by the time I got home, so I didn't get to enjoy the scenery except on the weekends."

"Did you get outside on the weekends?" Tasker Lake had a good reputation for ice fishing, but Eleanor wouldn't want to do that alone.

"No, not much. Saturday was nice, with that pretty

snowfall. I just curled up with a good book and watched it snow. Later, I did some shoveling while Uncle Gary came by and plowed. Three days later, here I am, living with my great aunt. It's not in town, though—about ten minutes outside of Milaca." She grimaced. "It's going to be a longer commute to work every day."

That gorgeous day, on the lake, and she stayed inside to look at it through the window? "Do you ski? I went out on Platke Lake Saturday, cross-country."

"Are the lakes frozen enough for that?" She looked alarmed.

"Platke is, and Tasker would be, but not all of them."

"I went cross-country skiing a few times, back home," Eleanor said, "but more downhill. Nothing impressive... just Minnesota mountains." She grinned. "It's not like going to Aspen or Vail. Anyhow, I probably would have moved to town soon, even if he hadn't been hurt. He likes to use the cabin. He and his friends used it for opening weekend—deer season—and I went to visit my parents, but I can't do that every time he wants to use his own cabin. He stayed out there when I was in the cities for Christmas, snowmobiling and maybe ice fishing. He put out his ice fishing house, so I knew he wanted to go fishing. I felt guilty."

"I can see how that might get awkward," David said.

"He kept telling me I didn't have to leave, but... Aunt Violet wanted me to come live with her, and now I have a bedroom in her house, with not much privacy at all, so I kind of miss the cabin."

"Are you there long-term?" Was that a sufficiently-tactful way of asking if she planned to stay around? He wanted someone ready to settle down. "In the area, I mean?"

"I'm... well, I want to stay here. I think I'll like it here, once I get settled in." She met his eyes. "Part of the reason I signed up at Betwixt Two Hearts is that I haven't met anyone but Brittany and my family. I love them, but I need some other friends."

Friends. He appreciated her honesty, but... friends? Maybe she found it awkward to talk about looking for a husband with a stranger. "You like it here?"

"I do. To tell you the truth," she said, "I didn't know if I would, but I wanted to leave the cities and do something different. Not teaching."

"Not teaching? Couldn't you not teach there?"

"No, I couldn't not teach there." She propped her elbows on the table, resting her chin on her clasped hands. "I come from a very academically-inclined family. They all think education is the only worthwhile occupation in the world. When I left my job, my parents—and my brothers—took it personally. They even wanted me to see a counselor. I love my family, but I needed to get out of town if I wanted to not teach."

"They wanted you to see a counselor?" David asked. "Just because you didn't want to be a teacher?"

She hunched her shoulders in a shrug. "They figured I must be depressed or have some other issue. They kept suggesting things like changing schools or grade levels or finding another job within the system."

"But you didn't want to do that?"

"No."

David needed time to think. She certainly didn't sound settled; she sounded like she ran away from home and didn't know what she wanted to do next. He pulled his phone from his pocket and tapped the screen. "Hey, it's after ten. I hope your uncle won't mind if you're late. At least he can't fire you, right?"

9

I heard you had an accident!"

"Hi, Brittany." Eleanor tapped the speaker button. "Not me. It was Uncle Gary. He fell, getting out of his truck."

"I heard you were bleeding and near hypothermia."

"Aunt Violet?" Eleanor asked.

"Nope, my friend Amy is on the EMT squad. I was a little hurt that I had to get the news from someone else."

She did sound hurt. Eleanor lifted a stack of books from her stool and sat. "I'm sorry, Brittany. I would have called if I was hurt, but really, I just sort of scraped my head, and it bled all over the place. Or rather, all over my hair and face, so I looked like the victim in a horror film. But it didn't need stitches or anything. And hypothermia... that one might be true. I was crawling around on the wet ice under Uncle Gary's truck, trying to find the keys to the office."

"Brrr. That must have been awful. How's your uncle?"

"Not bad, all things considered," Eleanor replied. "He's moving to a rehab facility tomorrow. But I do want to tell you what else happened on Monday. You won't believe it."

"Tell me! Or would you rather meet for lunch and

tell me there?"

Eleanor picked up the list Uncle Gary had dictated to her. "I've got to stay here to accept some deliveries and answer the phones. Why don't you come here? I can show you what I do!"

"Okay. Did you bring a lunch, or should I stop for something on the way?"

"Aunt Violet packed me a lunch. I have peanut butter sandwiches and apple slices, like a second-grader."

When Brittany's eyes glazed, Eleanor took pity on her and rolled up the blueprints. "I suppose it's not wildly exciting, but I enjoy it."

"You do? You'd rather do this than teaching?"

"Yes. I'm really enjoying it. There's something satisfying about it. Uncle Gary can do anything. He does a lot of energy projects and plumbing and pipes and metal construction... making things work. Look at this." Eleanor picked up the photo from her uncle's desk. "This is a little pavilion out at Meyer Park. It uses solar and wind power together for lights and to operate this little sculpture thing."

"I've seen that. That's more interesting than plumbing, anyhow."

"This one was designed by David Reid." She waited for the name to register. Apparently, it didn't. "David Reid! My match from the Betwixt Two Hearts agency!"

"Oh! He works with your uncle? Have you met him yet? Again, I mean?"

"I did, right here, on Monday morning, when I was

soaking wet and covered with blood!"

Brittany dropped her McDonalds bag on the table. "He was here?"

Eleanor nodded. "He had an appointment with Uncle Gary. He got here before the ambulance did. And he recognized me, even like that!" She lowered her voice. "And when I mentioned that yesterday, he said, 'I would know you anywhere.' I couldn't decide at first, if that was creepy or romantic, but he's a nice guy."

"Wait, wait. What happened yesterday? It's only been about three days since I talked to you last, and you've moved into town, nearly died of hypothermia, met your guy twice, and started running your uncle's company! You move fast!"

"Me?" Eleanor laughed. "I'm not a fast mover, but it has been an eventful week. And don't let Uncle Gary hear you say that about his business. He's all worked up. He gave me a list of things he wants me to bring him at the rehab center. It's going to look like mobile command center."

"That should go over well with the staff. You want some french fries?"

"Thanks. We met again at the hospital yesterday and had coffee. He's a nice guy."

"Okay," said Brittany, "you've said that twice. Are you trying to convince me or yourself?"

"No, really, he is. He seems like just a nice, ordinary guy." Eleanor unwrapped her sandwich, folding the waxed paper into quarters before putting it back in the lunchbox. Any discomfort she'd experienced was her own fault. Hedging the truth on an online questionnaire—gaming the algorithm—had seemed so simple before she had to sit down with David and explain things.

"Was he very analytical? Penny says engineers can lack people skills that way—Brian being the exception, of course."

"Of course." Eleanor sipped her water. "How can two people, who've known each other all their lives, be so besotted?"

"Right? I'm trying to think of a really sappy wedding gift for them. His & Hers embroidered bathrobes or something like that."

"Oh, that reminds me! You won't believe this." Eleanor broke off self-consciously. "Sorry. You don't want to hear my family drama."

"Sure, I do!" Brittany pointed a fry at her. "I'm saving up credits. My family is pretty drama-free at the moment, but our time will come. I'm all ears."

"Laurie called on Monday morning. She's talking about presents now, like they're getting married, only bigger."

"Bigger than wedding gifts? Like what?"

"Trips to the Caribbean."

Brittany dropped her hamburger and stared. "Trips...plural?"

"No, only one to the islands. I believe Soren is sending them to Chicago, to see a show and visit the art museums."

"Cheapskate."

"No, that would be me," Eleanor said. "I wasn't planning to give them a gift at all."

Brittany picked up her hamburger. "So, what are you going to give them?"

"Not a clue. A dozen roses might be in my budget. Maybe."

"How about making them something?"

"Like what?" Eleanor asked. "I'm not real crafty. I could look on Pinterest, but really... it's hard to compete with sandy beaches. Not that I want to compete," she added hastily. "I just don't want to look like an idiot or an ungrateful, rebellious daughter."

"Can you paint? How about photography? You could take a nice picture of scenery or something from your mom's childhood and have it framed."

"I don't have a camera." Eleanor picked up her phone. "This takes pretty good pictures, but I'm not sure I could print anything really big."

"How about a quilt? Your aunt could help you. Or you could knit or crochet an afghan if you don't want to do a quilt."

"Knitting and crocheting were not included in my extensive education. In fact," Eleanor said, "I don't think I had any really creative classes. Academic classes, some music and sports. I can play volleyball and the piano. Soccer and basketball, too, but I went to school on a volleyball scholarship."

"I didn't know that!" Brittany leaned forward and propped her elbows on the table. "Where did you go to college?"

"Rockland University."

"Oh, I know where that is! It's a big engineering school, isn't it?"

"That and education. Guess which one I went to." Eleanor smiled tightly. "After a few months here, I'm beginning to think I should have gone into engineering. Doing take-offs isn't the same thing as engineering, of course, but it's related, and I think I'm better at that than I am at teaching."

"Did you have a boyfriend down there?"

"A boyfriend? No."

"No? None at all?"

Eleanor wrinkled her nose. "Like you said, it was a lot of engineering. Penny's absolutely right about them. Have you ever dated an engineer or scientist?"

"No, I haven't," Brittany said. "I think Brian's the only engineer I know."

"Well—except for Brian, of course—they aren't the most romantic men on earth. I went out to the theater with one guy, and he whispered through the whole performance, telling me which color lights were being used and why. I mean the whole performance—not just a few comments. Not only was it annoying, but our neighbors were furious. I can't remember the last time I was so embarrassed. Then he asked me to go to a concert the following weekend. I figured that would be okay, since it was outdoors—no lights. But then he just talked about sound waves, through the whole thing."

Brittany grinned. "Did you go out with him again?"

"No, but he kept trying. He said he'd really enjoyed our time together."

"So, don't date an engineer."

"Actually," Eleanor said, "the scientists were just as bad. My roommate set me up with her boyfriend's roommate, thinking that would be convenient for them. He was a good-looking guy, and I thought a zoologist would be interesting, but he spent the entire date talking about the life cycle of the dung beetle. Not kidding. I didn't ask about dung beetles. We didn't see a bug that inspired conversation. We sat down at the restaurant, got our water, and Heath said, 'Have you ever seen a dung beetle?' I thought it was a joke at first, so I said no and waited for the punch line. There wasn't one."

"A dung beetle? What's a dung beetle?"

"Just what you'd expect. He started at conception and worked his way through the beetle's life until the poor thing died and dried up. Seriously, the entire meal. It was like he couldn't help himself. He just kept talking. I could tell he was miserable when he said goodbye and dropped me off."

Brittany laughed. "Poor guy. He was probably nervous."

"I hope he became a professor, because he was a good lecturer. To this day, I remember most of what he told me. I didn't have a lot of time for dating, though. Like I said, I was there on a volleyball scholarship, and we practiced off-season, too. I had a heavy class load, because I wanted to get through my double master's degree in five years, and my sorority activities, too. I didn't have time for other socializing."

"I only went to the community college," Brittany said. "It was fun. I got an associate's degree in marketing and business by the time I was 19, and I've been doing this ever since. I worked for the newspaper for a while, but now I'm keeping busy and making more money freelancing. I like it." She held out the carton. "Want some more fries? I got the large one, to share, and then I ate almost all of them myself."

"No thanks. Where did you meet your fiancé?"

"At school. He works at the car dealership south of town, in the shop."

"When are you getting married?"

"No hurry." Brittany popped the last fry in her mouth and rolled up her garbage. "We haven't set a date. We were planning on Christmas—this coming Christmas—but not a specific day. That's how I met Penny.

I took my wedding dress designs to her, and she asked me to do her social media and marketing. Where should I put this?"

Eleanor pointed to the garbage can. "So, you have a dress but not a wedding date?"

"Well, I told Penny to hold off on the dress, too."

"That doesn't sound good."

Brittany sat and looked at her. "My sister just got a divorce. It made me take a good look at what I wanted in a man—in marriage. I asked Andy if we could go to premarital counseling, and he laughed. He wouldn't do it." She shrugged. "I decided I wanted a man who was willing to go to premarital counseling. Our pastor says that it's an investment in marriage, and if a man isn't willing to make that small investment ahead of time, he might not be willing to invest much later—to do whatever it takes to fix things if there's a problem. When Andy made a joke of it and said it would be a waste of time... well, that was a red flag. I'm not breaking off the engagement—at least, not now—but I'm praying for wisdom. And maybe some courage.

10

W ell, that stinks." Eleanor sat in the hard chair next to the bed. "I mean, I understand they have to have a deadline, but it was a big project, and your bid was good. All that time wasted!"

"You did a good job on it," Gary said, "and it wasn't a waste of time, because you learned while you worked. Each project is more practice, like playing the piano."

She laughed. "Like playing the piano?"

"Yeah. You play the piano, don't you? I seem to remember your mother talking about your recitals when I was down there for her fortieth birthday party."

"I haven't done it in a while, but yes, I can play. Why?"

He plucked at the blanket. "I have a favor to ask. Don't be afraid to say no." He paused. "Well, if you say no, you'll have to explain it to Aunt Violet, but if you'd really rather not, I'll figure something else out."

"What?"

"On Tuesdays, over at the nursing home where Uncle Olof is..." He stopped. "Actually, it's a rehabilitation center, and I'll be there, too, while this leg heals up. So, on Tuesday mornings, they have sing-alongs. They sing old songs, from when they were younger."

"Okay." She waited. Did he want her to play

accompaniment?

"Well, I'm not going to be able to play for a while, with this shoulder, and I'd very much appreciate it if you'd fill in for me." The last few words came out in a rush.

"You mean, you play the piano for their sing-alongs?"

"Yeah. It's not hard. I can't do concertos, but Cheryl had a piano, and she taught me how to bang out a few songs. They aren't a picky audience."

She smiled at him, amused and a little surprised by the affection she felt for this uncle she hadn't known until a few months ago. "And you want me to do it?"

"I'd be grateful if you would. I'd still pay you for 8 hours on Tuesdays, plus all the overtime you'll be collecting for the next few weeks. If you have an early lunch, you could be at the office by 12:30."

"Well, what songs would I have to play?" Did she really want to do this? Did she have a choice? "I haven't played in a while."

"I have songbooks. It's old stuff—'When Irish Eyes are Smiling', 'Don't Sit Under the Apple Tree', 'When You Wore a Tulip', 'Yellow Rose of Texas'.... "

"I don't know any of those," Eleanor objected.

"You will," Gary said darkly. "They're the kind of songs that get stuck in your head, and the next thing you know, you're humming 'A Bicycle Built for Two' on the job site."

"Good morning!" Cheryl rolled a wheelchair ahead of her as she entered. "Hi, Eleanor. No need to leave. I just want to see him get in and out of the wheelchair."

"I thought I wasn't supposed to do that." Gary sat up, pivoting to dangle his legs over the side of the bed. "I thought I had to wait for assistance."

"That is correct. Both here and at the nursing home, you must wait for a CNA or nurse to assist you in or out of your chair or bed."

"Then why do you want me to do it now?"

His exaggerated patience didn't put a dent in her cheerful demeanor. "Because, Gary, you are going to do it anyhow, and I want to make sure you know how to do it without injuring yourself all over again."

Eleanor giggled. No wonder Aunt Violet liked this woman.

Gary grinned ruefully. "Oh, no. I'm going to follow every rule to the T, so I can get out of that place and back to work."

"I don't think so. Have you seen the CNA's at the nursing home? You're going to have to call them when you want to use the bathroom, Gary, or just to get out of bed in the morning."

He scowled at her. "Would you please stop calling it a nursing home? It's a rehabilitation center."

Cheryl pursed her lips and tilted her head, considering. "No, I don't think so. I like calling it a nursing home."

"You could call it a rehab clinic, Uncle Gary," Eleanor said, "but then people would think you were there to break a drug habit."

"In and out of the chair, Gary. I'm not signing off on your discharge until I see you do it."

He heaved a sigh. "Did you come back here just to torment me?"

"No," Cheryl said, "that's not why I came back. It is a nice little bonus, though. Just wait until we get to the nursing home, where we'll have more time together." She smiled with all her teeth. "We'll get you fixed up in no time."

Later that afternoon, as she drove out to the office, Eleanor realized she was humming "A Bicycle Built for Two" and burst into laughter. All those years of piano lessons were finally going to be put to good use. What would her mother think?

"Your mother will be pleased." Violet beamed at Eleanor she set a cup and saucer on the table. "You remember, I told you how fond of him she was. They sang songs together, possibly some of the same ones you'll be playing on Tuesdays."

Eleanor still had trouble believing in that relationship. If her mother had ever mentioned Olof, it was only in passing or in connection with the rest of the family.

"And she read to him. He'd work while she read, or sometimes he'd sit with her and look at the pages as if he could read, too. He couldn't, you know. He has dyslexia, like Penny, but no one ever knew that back then. Teachers just thought he was lazy. It wasn't until Penny was diagnosed that the doctors tested him."

"I didn't know that."

"Your mother—as far as I know—never asked him

to read to her. She read and he listened." Violet tipped her head and looked at Eleanor. "Does anyone else in your family have dyslexia?"

Eleanor shook her head. "No, not that I know of. The twins are just three. Of course, they'll be starting preschool soon, and Laurie will want them reading by the time they're four, so I guess we'll find out. Dyslexia is hereditary, isn't it? I wonder if Mom worried about that."

Violet spread butter on her roll. "It's hereditary, at least a bit, but it's hard to tell how much, because when you go back a generation or two, we didn't know about it. We just thought people weren't smart enough to learn. They were just labeled illiterate."

"That's sad." Eleanor stirred sugar into her coffee. She might as well take advantage of her aunt's good mood. "Speaking of my mother... are you going to my parents' anniversary party?"

"Oh, I don't think so," Violet said. "I'll send them a card."

That seemed an appropriate response to a 35th anniversary. Eleanor wished she could do the same. "Laurie, Zack's wife, thinks we should give them gifts. Us kids, I mean."

"What kind of gifts?"

"Expensive gifts. Soren's giving them a weekend in Chicago, to see a show. Zack and Laurie are giving them a vacation in the Caribbean." Eleanor blew out a sigh. "I don't know what to give them."

Violet sat upright. "A vacation in the Caribbean!

What will you give them for their fiftieth—a new car?"

"Thank you. I agree, but I'm stuck. I can't afford something like that. Brittany suggested making a quilt for them, but I don't know how to do it, and from what I've seen here, it requires a lot of tools I don't have. Would you be willing to help me make one, if it's even possible to get one made by Valentine's Day?"

Would this be a good time to start humming "A Bicycle Built for Two"?

"Do you think they would like a quilt?" Violet asked.

"I think so. Mom likes handcrafted things as long as they aren't too hokey. I saw some quilts on Pinterest that looked kind of modern. Is fabric expensive?"

"Sometimes," Violet said. "We can find a sale and coupons. I'll help you if you're sure you want to do it. And I'll show you how to use the quilting machine."

"That's a little intimidating!" Relieved, Eleanor leaned back in her chair. "I appreciate it. It won't be as nice as the other gifts, but at least it's better than a bouquet of flowers or a gift certificate to a restaurant they could afford better than I can."

"I'm sure she'll like it. They both will. Do you have time to look at patterns after work today?"

"Yes, I can do that." She picked up her phone and navigated to Pinterest. "Let me show you what I found. I'm completely open to suggestions, though."

"Can you get my reading glasses from my nightstand for me? I can't see those little screens."

When Eleanor returned, her aunt was reading her text messages—apparently without the aid of her readers. She looked up without a trace of embarrassment. "Brittany wants to know how your date went. Were you on a date? I didn't know you have a young man here."

"I didn't go on a date." Not yet. Eleanor reached for the phone.

Violet released it. "You don't have to keep secrets from me. I'm not your chaperon. At your age, you ought to be dating. You're even older than Penny."

Amusement swept away Eleanor's irritation. "I'm not that old."

"You're not that young, either," the woman said tartly. "You don't want to be my age and still have kids underfoot."

The idea staggered the imagination. Eleanor couldn't help laughing. "No, I don't. But I still have a few good childbearing years left." She tapped in a quick message to Brittany and closed the text window. "Here's the first quilt I saw. It's called a double wedding ring, so it seemed appropriate."

"It would take six months and a lot of skill," Violet said. "You need one that can be rotary cut and machine pieced quickly."

"I don't know which ones those would be. How about this one?"

"We could do that one." Her aunt took the phone and scrolled down the page. "Do you have certain colors in mind?"

"The house is pretty neutral. A lot of white now that us kids are all gone. I thought maybe I could make it for Valentine's Day, but not too country-style."

"The style won't matter as much as the fabrics you choose," her aunt said absently. "Since you said seasonal, are you talking about a wall hanging or a lap quilt instead of a bed quilt?"

"Yes. I don't want to interfere with their bedroom

decor." Eleanor fought the urge to snatch her phone back. "Something for the couch or to hang on the wall somewhere."

"How about this? It looks like Swedish paper baskets." Aunt Violet turned the phone so Eleanor could see it but didn't let go. "It has hearts, so it would work for Valentine's Day or a wedding anniversary. We could look at different fabrics, but I like the moderate contrast here."

Eleanor looked up at the suddenly authoritative voice. Aunt Violet knew what she was doing.

"Not beige, since you said their house is white, but maybe in grays? With some pink or blue?" She handed the phone to Eleanor. "I'll draft it out, and we can go shopping tomorrow."

11

Violet

Now that she'd given her spare room to Eleanor, there wasn't space to dedicate to her genealogy and family history projects. Violet dragged the last tote into the middle of the quilting room. The annex, with its four bedrooms, should have been more than enough space for her, but after years of living in other people's houses, she reveled in being able to spread out.

"Hey! I can do that!" Eleanor sounded more alarmed than the circumstances warranted. Violet appreciated help; she didn't like being treated like a frail old lady.

"Thank you, Nellie." She pulled off the lid of the tote and straightened, rubbing her hip. "I thought maybe you could use this room for the transcriptions and editing. We can bring in a desk and chair for you."

Eleanor walked to the quilting machine and ran her hand over Violet's current project. "This one is smaller than the other ones I've seen. I like the colors."

Too small. This quilt had been the hardest. It should have been bigger, to record a long life with a wife and family. Instead, it was small and... lonely. Who would want a quilt made for a boy who'd died at 19 years old, nearly

75 years ago? She joined Eleanor and touched at the small flag and cross.

"Karl didn't live long enough to fill up a bigger quilt. He died in 1944, in Normandy." She pointed. "Those blocks record the rest of us, and our parents and grandparents, but there wasn't much to say about his own life."

"He was your brother?"

"Yes, my favorite." She smiled, remembering the many kindnesses of her older brother. They'd etched themselves into her mind—her heart—over the decades, and she'd written them in his book, not wanting Karl to be lost. She and Olof were the only people who remembered Karl now, and poor Olof's memories grew fuzzier every day.

She turned to Eleanor. "This is what I need your help with. All these journals..." Violet gestured at the tote. "They need to be typed up. I wrote those out by hand, before I had a typewriter. The blue tote has typed pages that need to be re-typed into the computer, and what's already in the computer needs to be edited and organized."

Eleanor's eyes widened. "All that is family history?"

"We've been around since 1908," Violet said. "In America, anyways. I didn't record much about the time before that. Do you think you can do it?" She couldn't leave it in this kind of mess. She'd been entrusted with these stories, and even if no one else cared, she had to get them recorded for posterity—whether posterity wanted them or not.

"I'll do my best. That's a lot of history!"

"Four generations of Anderson family life," Violet said. "But the fourth generation is starting to multiply faster than I can sew or write, so I'm falling behind. Will this room work for you?"

"This is your quilting room! Can't I just do it at the kitchen table or in the living room? I can carry my laptop computer anywhere."

"Are you sure?" Violet asked. "If you're sure, we could keep these totes in a corner of the living room, and you can just take out what you need." Relief lightened her spirits. As important as the written history was, Violet craved the time alone in this room, with God and her history quilts, rolling back and forth along the quilt, guiding the head of the quilting machine, humming and praying silently—and sometimes, not so silently. She'd have to remember there was another person in the house. She didn't want to startle Eleanor.

"It's working out great. I'm loving Aunt Violet. She's telling me all sorts of stories about you."

Violet leaned in, grateful for the annex's modern doors, so unlike the solid wood ones in the main part of the farmhouse. Eleanor was silent for a few minutes, and she eased back, hoping she hadn't been detected. It must be Kathy. Too bad the girl didn't use speaker phone.

"No, really. It's nice here. I have your old bedroom, and even your old dresser, with lilac shelf paper in the drawers. You should see the lilac trees that you and Uncle Olof planted. They're huge! He remembered planting them, too."

Eleanor continued after a shorter pause. "He's good. Aunt Violet says it was one of his good days. He looks like a much older version of Uncle Gary."

Kathy must have had more to say this time. Violet could hear Eleanor moving around the room, opening and shutting drawers, sitting on the bed and walking over the squeaky floorboard by the window.

When she started talking again, her voice was sharper. "That's why I have to stay here, Mom. My job didn't go away because Gary's not there. He needs me now, to do a lot more than just the takeoffs and some office work. I'm getting to do some of what he usually does. He's teaching me about the business, and I'm liking it!"

A brief wait this time. "I know you love me, Mom, and you want what's best for me, but I like it here. I like my job, and I like this part of our family. Oh! I forgot to tell you. On Tuesday mornings, I'm going to be playing the piano for the golden oldies sing-along at the nursing home where Uncle Olof and Gary are. Did you know Gary was doing that until he got hurt?"

It sounded like the call was ending. Violet stepped away, ready to slip into her own room, just catching Eleanor's next words.

"I'll be there. I wish you'd come here for a visit, though. Everyone would love to see you. Just think about it, okay? I love you. Bye."

"Good morning, Aunt Violet!"

Violet leaned in to receive Constance's hug. "Good morning, dear. Eleanor's parking the car. She dropped me off in front."

"There she is." Brian smiled at Eleanor. "I'm glad the two of you made it, in this weather."

113

"Oh, yes," Violet said. "We wouldn't miss church." She was going to make sure Eleanor didn't miss church, as long as the girl was staying with her.

"The church is always full when there's a blizzard," Penny said. "Everyone has to demonstrate their hardiness and devotion."

"And they're not above calling the slackers to ask why they missed church," her fiancé put in.

"It's pride." Violet handed him her tote bag so she could shed her coat. "It's not just going to church in the blizzard but also making sure everyone sees you strapping on your snowshoes."

"I'd be pretty proud of myself if I had to wear snowshoes to get to church," Eleanor said. "Aunt Violet was telling me about going to the old church in the winter, when everyone lived in the farmhouse. It sounds a lot harder than just driving my nice warm car down a plowed highway, and they had perfect attendance!"

Everyone looked at Violet, and she felt her cheeks warming. Maybe she'd exaggerated a teensy bit, but it wasn't pride to take pride ... er, to be glad that one's family had a good attendance record.

"Anyhow, whatever their true motivation, the church is present and on time during bad weather." Penny hooked her arm through Brian's.

The sermon was on pride. Penny leaned across Eleanor to point out the information in the bulletin and jerked her hand away when Violet slapped it.

"Shh. Sit still." She heard the stifled giggles and was tempted to pinch them, as she had their parents for such behavior.

"Hello, Olof."

"Hello." He extended a hand, and Violet shook it. Another one of those days. The good ones were getting further apart. At least he'd been able to talk to Eleanor last week. Maybe, if Kathy came, he'd remember her.

"Would you like to go down to the living room? There's a little girl looking for someone to play checkers with. Do you like checkers?"

"She cheats." Olof handed her a book. "Have you read this?"

"Yes, it's a good book." It was an old TV guide. She set it on the dresser and wheeled him to the lobby, praying he wouldn't be overwhelmed by the visitors. Most of the elderly residents lacked company; Olof had enough for all of them.

He spied Sarah, of course, and ignored the rest of them. "Violet! What are you doing over there? We need to go home."

"I want to play checkers."

He wavered. "We need to go home."

"Come on." Sarah got behind the wheelchair and pushed him toward one of the game tables. "Let's play checkers."

"Okay, but no cheating." He placed the checkers in one long row on his side of the board. "Is that right?"

"Let me fix it." Eleanor stepped close and tried to adjust them. "They alternate, on the black squares."

He slapped at her hands. "I can do it! Violet and I are playing checkers. Go away. Go home."

Violet hoped Eleanor's feelings wouldn't be hurt.

She'd had to grow an extra layer of skin herself in the last year or two, as Olof's filter deteriorated. "Be nice, Olof. This is Eleanor. We're going to watch TV for a while."

"Bye." He didn't take his eyes off the board.

"Why does he call Sarah Violet?" Eleanor asked. "Does he think she's you? I read a bit about Alzheimer's after our last visit here, and the article said what you did — he thinks he's a child, looking for his mom or wanting to go home."

Eleanor had researched it. Violet patted her arm. "Exactly. He's not always in the past, though. Sometimes when we come, he recognizes me but not her, so I introduce her as Sarah, and he's nice to her. Sometimes he doesn't remember either of us." She nodded at the wing chairs. "We can keep an eye on them from here. Carl and Constance went down to check on Gary. On days like today, he's eight years old. If I tell him I'm Violet, he doesn't believe me, because I'm an old lady. To him, Violet is his little sister."

"And Sarah just plays along? That's kind of... creepy."

"Ha." Penny spoke from behind Violet. "You don't know Sarah. She would play games with anyone—any game—24 hours a day, if she could, and she's always loved Uncle Olof."

"When she was little," Violet said, "I think she loved him because he couldn't get away from her. She'd push him around in his wheelchair wherever she wanted to go or climb in his lap and read books to him, long before she could actually read the words. It's just how she knew him." That was a while ago, though. He was so unpredictable now.

"It's my turn. You just went." Sarah pushed at

Olof's hand. The old man grumbled but complied, waiting for the girl to move her checker.

"Okay, you can go now."

"She's competitive, too," Penny commented. "She's not going to let him win."

"Is it always this empty?" Eleanor asked.

"Most of the residents take a nap in the afternoon. Olof doesn't." Violet shifted in her chair, avoiding the stare of an elderly man in high-waisted jeans and suspenders. The collar of his plaid shirt stood out around his skinny neck, not shifting with the movement of his head as he strutted toward them. He'd stalked her last time she was here, too.

Sarah jumped two of Olof's checkers, and her crow of triumph rang through the room, drawing indulgent smiles and a few sleepy mutters.

"Hopefully, I'll never have to be here," Violet said. "Thanks to Penny, I have a home at the farmhouse as long as I need it. She and Brian are going to live there for a little while, and then they might rent it out to one of his sisters. So, there will be someone around."

"We won't leave you there alone," Penny said.

"When are you getting married?" Eleanor asked. "I haven't heard a date yet."

"We wanted a spring wedding, so we can have it outside, but the more I'm around brides and their mothers, the more I want to elope."

"Too many mosquitoes in the spring, and you can't trust the weather. "Violet turned a shoulder to the man, praying he was just passing by. "And you can't elope. You've put too much into this bridal business of yours. You have to have a nice wedding. It won't hurt you to wait a few months."

"The shop is amazing." Eleanor glanced at the man and back to Penny. "You'd never guess from the outside what it's like inside. I went with my college roommate to a bridal shop in Chicago. It was so elegant we were afraid to touch anything. Yours is elegant, but it's more comfortable.

"Country chic." Violet said. "That's what she calls it. It does look nice."

"Thank you. Dad will finish up the landscaping in the spring, and in a year or two, when it's all grown in, it'll be a showcase. First impressions matter, you know, especially with mothers of brides, who are expecting to pay a thousand dollars for a wedding dress."

"Ole, what are you doing over here?" A middle-aged woman in Tinker Bell scrubs hurried toward them. "This is Miss Anderson. She's Olof's sister."

"Ja." He spit the word out. "It's her... da sister. Da hussy. Traitor." Violet pressed back in her chair, frightened by his venom. His toothless mouth and thick accent garbled the words, but there was no mistaking the hate. He leaned closer. "Tramp! You're out dere in da field, consortin vit Jerry -"

"Ole! Stop that! I'm so sorry, Miss Anderson. Come on, Ole." The aide raised her voice. "Mary! Can you come help me?"

Violet's breathing slowed as the man turned his anger on his caregivers.

"What was that about?" Eleanor stared after them. "Do they have violent patients here?"

"Are you okay, Aunt Violet?" Penny crouched in front of her.

No, she wasn't okay. She'd never been called a tramp before. The absurdity of the accusations finally brought a chuckle. "I'm fine. I don't know who Jerry is, but

I promise, I'm not consorting with him or anyone else, especially in a field in January."

12

David picked out the elegant, simple melody of "King on a Donkey" as the ushers passed the communion plates. Angela Ridgewell sat at the end of the back row, alone, staring out the window. Had she heard the message about extravagant grace? He should mention her to Pastor Jack, so he could follow up.

Or was that his responsibility? He could ask one of the women to do it, but a pastor couldn't shirk fifty percent of his work because he didn't want to minister to women — or more specifically, a particular woman. In public, in the company of the rest of the church, he couldn't use discretion and "best practices" as excuses. He just didn't want to do it. Honesty counted for something, right?

He brought the song to an end as the ushers returned the plates. The closing song, "Grace Greater Than Our Sin", with its catchy waltz rhythm, might touch Angela, unless the bloody parts bothered her. He caved in on the last line. The woman was here, all by herself, and he had the Gospel to share.

"We'll meet you at Charcoal Grill. We know you've

got people to talk to, and your dad and I could use some coffee."

Confirmation. David made his way down the side aisle and stopped at the sight of Angela in conversation with Larry. His friend sat in the aisle ahead of her, turned around, listening to whatever Angela was saying. Maybe he'd be at the restaurant sooner than he'd thought. Even as he turned to go, she stood and strode away. Larry, rose, brows drawn together, rubbing the back of his neck.

"How'd it go?" David waited for Larry to exit the row. "What did she think of the service?"

"Angela? She didn't say."

"She was talking to you!"

"People do that," Larry said. "Even people who aren't my clients."

"She must have said something about it." David looked at the other man, exasperated. "I was hoping she heard the sermon. She really needs the Lord."

Larry stopped walking and turned around. David rocked back, to avoid a collision.

"In all your classes, at UMD and in this seminary, do you have any classes in human psychology? How do you plan to be a counselor? Just read Bible verses at people and tell them to suck it up and trust God?" He grabbed David's elbow and pulled him through the crowd, into the library. "She needs Jesus, but I think she needs something else, too."

David opened his mouth to argue, but Larry held up a hand. "He is sufficient, but guess what... He uses me, too, and other kinds of doctors."

He'd never seen Larry angry before. David dropped into a chair. "Yes, He does. What do you mean about Angela?"

"Something's going on. I don't like to interfere, and if she was my patient, I couldn't. But I've known her since we were kids. I might go talk to Meg. Cal won't get it, and I don't know if Meg will. They're both pretty single-minded." He sat opposite David. "Their mother was a mess. Still is, as far as I know." He chuckled. "That's not a professional opinion—just my childhood memories of her."

David leaned forward. "You mean she's suicidal or on drugs or something? A mental illness?"

"I don't know." Larry stood and extended a hand to pull David to his feet. "You going to lunch with your mom and dad?"

"They're waiting for me at Charcoal Grill."

"By the way, have you met your match yet?" Larry grinned at his joke. "Were you able to overcome that unfortunate first impression?"

"Yes! It's a long story, but we have a date for Tuesday night. I think it's going pretty well."

"How can it be a long story? Didn't you just get her information a week ago?"

"It's been an eventful week." David pulled on his coat. "Don't worry. I'm not rushing things." He shrugged. "There are a couple things—not red flags, but maybe yellow. Like a traffic light."

"My mom thinks a yellow light means you should accelerate to get through before it turns red," Larry said. "Personally, I step on my brakes at that point."

"I'm somewhere in between. I'll proceed with caution." Maybe it would be better to step on the brakes, though, and wait for a green light. God's green light.

David liked scholarly Old Testament sermons, but this professor managed to turn vibrant, God-breathed history into dusty lists and statistics. He closed the laptop and propped his feet on the coffee table. It was all important, even the genealogies and numbers, gruesome deaths and family history—much of it dysfunctional. God included it in Scripture, after all. He wrote it all out, in great detail, and then He repeated it in Chronicles. Professor Voe expected David to memorize all of it.

Tomorrow night, he'd talk to Eleanor about her faith. She'd been vague, and Christians weren't supposed to be vague. Had his profile made his intentions clear enough? Being a pastor's wife would be different from being an engineer's wife. He tried to picture her as a pastor's wife. He tried to picture himself as a pastor. The two of them, with a quiverful of little PK's, all dressed up and shiny on Sunday morning.

It didn't float, and he didn't think the children were the problem.

David leaned back and covered his face with his hands. He wanted to serve God, more than anything else, with all his being. He wanted it more than he wanted a wife and family... more than he wanted anything the world could provide. But lately, whenever he worked toward that goal, there was something in his path. His grandma would call it "a check in his spirit." Pastor Jack might call it spiritual warfare.

Which was it? Was he going down the wrong path, with the Holy Spirit trying to redirect him, or was he on the right path, with Satan trying to stop him?

"Even the ones who don't talk were singing!" Eleanor lifted a stack of papers from a chair and set them on her desk. "You can sit here. I'm trying to stay on top of the things I can do here. Uncle Gary is so positive and encouraging, but he must be worried. We missed a deadline the day after the accident, and now we're trying to coordinate things between here and the nursing home and the job sites."

"Are you going out to job sites?" Brittany grinned. "I can just picture you with a yellow hard hat. You could take a selfie and send it to your sister-in-law. But tell me about your sing-along. I've read about music therapy for dementia patients. How does it work?"

"I play the piano and they sing. I thought I'd have to lead singing, but Gary did it. They all came into the living room in their wheelchairs, an aide handed out songbooks, and I played. They're all songs from the 20's, 30's, and 40's. We sang all the songs, and then they left.

She'd loved it. The best part—the very best—was Uncle Gary. He sang with gusto, waving his good arm as if directing a choir. He helped people turn the pages in their songbooks and introduced each song with enthusiasm. She could see why women were attracted to him. Gary Anderson was generous, easy-going, kind, and chivalrous. That's probably how he'd ended up married so many times. He'd given her this job even though she wasn't qualified and let her stay in his cabin. She had no doubt that if she'd made a mess of the take-offs, he'd have found her something else to do.

"Are you going to do it every week, then?" Brittany asked.

"That's the plan, until Uncle Gary is healed up."

"So... have you seen any more of David Reid?" Brittany took a bite of her salad. "Did you set up a real date?"

"Yes, as a matter of fact, we're going out to dinner tonight." She sat down opposite her friend. "I really like him, Brittany. He seems intelligent and sensible, and he's a good listener. He's good-looking, too, in a clean-cut, all-American kind of way."

"Meets all your qualifications, huh?"

Eleanor ignored the edge of sarcasm. "He does, and not just for the anniversary party." When he'd called to invite her to dinner, she'd forgotten all about the party. "I started thinking about that last night. It might be nice to get to know him and maybe even go out together, but I don't want a husband right now." It had kept her awake, listening to the wind, worrying about David's expectations. "He must have filled out the application because he wants a real relationship."

"Ya think?"

Eleanor dropped her gaze. "I know... I didn't think about him at all. I was so wrapped up in my own situation."

"How are you going to introduce the topic of your immediate need for a date on Valentine's Day, in Minneapolis? An overnight date, since I assume this party will last until at least midnight. You can't come back here that late."

"Sure, I can." She hadn't been planning to, though. She couldn't just take off like an ordinary guest.

"David may not want to drive back here late at

night, especially in winter," Brittany said.

"Then he can stay at my parents' house or get a hotel." The words lacked conviction, even in her own ears. Eleanor bit her lip. "It's a dinner. It can't go later than nine, can it?"

"I don't know how you folks do things down there in the big city," Brittany said with an exaggerated drawl, "but around here, we can stay up till midnight for a good party, especially if we're having a string quartet and a wine bar."

"Maybe I should just be honest with him," Eleanor said. She picked up her apple and set it down again. "But what if he gets mad and leaves?"

"Then you'll be right back where you started and have to decide whether or not you should just go to the party without a date. It wouldn't be the end of the world." Brittany wrinkled her nose. "My parents would rather have me come alone than get a date with a stranger just for the party."

"They wouldn't have to know he's a stranger," Eleanor muttered. "I don't need a date. It'll be fine. I'm making my family sound like monsters, and they aren't. Not at all. They're sincere, well-meaning people who love me and want the best for me."

"They sound egotistical and manipulative." Brittany bit into her sandwich.

"No, they're not!" But maybe a little, subconsciously. "I'm pinning my hopes on a blizzard. Let's talk about something else. Anything else."

"Oh, tell me about your quilt. Did you get the fabric?"

"Yes, and I like it. Aunt Violet really knows her stuff. She's got it all charted out and even printed out a picture of what it will look like. She has a program for designing quilts."

"I didn't know she was so computer-savvy," Brittany said.

"Oh, yes. She knows enough for what she wants to do—the quilts and her genealogy and writing. We're making a quilt with hearts on it. She's calling it a Swedehearts Glory Quilt."

"Swedehearts, like Swedish hearts? Why the Glory?"

"I'm not sure. She made one she called Christmas Glory for my aunt in Florida." Eleanor folded her paper napkin in half and then into quarters. "I don't always know what she's thinking. Sometimes she dithers around like an ordinary old lady, but she's sharper than most people give her credit for. She talks a lot about the family in her generation and the one after that—my mom's generation. I hadn't realized that my mom grew up there in the farmhouse, at least until she was ten. Aunt Violet's always talking about her."

"And then your mom went away to college and never came back. That's a common story in rural areas. Kids can't wait to leave the farm and move to the big city." Brittany licked her fingers. "Not me. It's fun to visit the cities for shopping or a special event, but I get all tense in traffic. And I like being able to see the stars at night."

"It's nice out here," Eleanor agreed, "especially in the winter. The snow stays whiter."

"We've had so much snow this year that it probably stays pretty white in the cities, too. It gets freshened up every day. Maybe you'll have your blizzard after all."

13

He always scanned both sides of the road for deer, watching for eyes reflecting the truck's headlights, but David never saw the one that raced from the woods straight into the side of his SUV. He recognized the jolting thud. Of all the rotten timing... why now? Grateful the plow had cleared the shoulder, he eased the truck to a stop.

The animal was nearly invisible in the dusk—a gray-brown lump in the middle of the road, where the next car was bound to hit it. Pulling on his gloves, he examined the damage to his truck. Stupid deer. Hopefully, it was dead, because he didn't have a way to put it out of its misery if it was suffering.

David pulled his phone from his pocket and turned on the flashlight app as he walked back toward the deer. He squatted by the still animal and shone his light over it. No visible blood; it must have broken its neck. One eye opened and glared at him. David groaned. Another time, he would have felt more compassion. Right now, he just wanted to drive away and not be late for his date with Eleanor.

He couldn't do it. David turned off the flashlight and put a hand on her heaving ribcage. Her eye closed. He stood up when the dispatcher answered. "Hi. This is David

Reid. I hit a deer out here on HWY 23, about 5 miles west of Milaca. Actually, she hit me. But I don't have a gun or anything, and she's still alive. Do you have someone who can come out and take care of her?"

The doe lifted her head and stared at him as if outraged. Three seconds later, she staggered to her feet, took a few dizzy steps, and then leaped off into the woods.

"Uh, never mind. She took off. She looks okay. Thanks anyhow."

Shaking his head, David got back in the SUV. He'd be late. Not a good start for a relationship, but surely Eleanor would understand; even in the city, people hit deer. He tapped out a message.

HIT A DEER. I'LL BE ABOUT TEN MINUTES LATE.

The response came immediately.

ARE YOU OKAY?

Nice. She cared.

THE DEER AND I ARE BOTH FINE. THE TRUCK HAS A DENT.

BE CAREFUL. SEE YOU SOON.

He smiled as he restarted the SUV. His mother said that—"be careful"—every time he left. He wished the Betwixt profile had some information about what kind of family Eleanor wanted. 2.5 children? Six? Maybe they could talk about that tonight, in a casual sort of way. No, there was nothing casual about conversations when you met through a matchmaking agency. Everything mattered.

Eleanor was drop-dead gorgeous and seemed like a nice person, but there was something confusing about her, too. He didn't even know if she was a Christian—at least, not really. She'd talked about church in a positive way and knew enough to be concerned about his doctrine, but... He'd have to ask her more openly tonight.

And what about her job—her career as a teacher? Was she just passing through here, restless and still trying to decide what she wanted in life? If so, why did she sign up for the matchmaking service? The goal of the agency was traditional marriage, not casual dating. Not friends.

David pushed the CD into the slot, and the sweet voice of Larry Norman filled the air. Edgy songs, more so than most contemporary Christian music, with blunt words of truth and calling Christians to love one another. To lift up the fallen and lost, instead of stepping over them. When some people were talking about free love, the Jesus People were telling everyone about the only real free love. David wished he'd been there, to see the Christian hippies and the men and women of the Jesus People movement, revolutionizing Christian culture in America. Evangelizing with abandon, his Grandma said. A grand adventure.

Eleanor sat on the bench to stop herself from pacing. He'd said he was fine, but how could you hit a deer and just continue on to a dinner date? She'd be a wreck, whether the deer was hurt or not. But if David hit it hard enough to put a dent in his truck, how could it be okay? At least he wouldn't arrive with it strapped to the top of his truck. She jumped to her feet and peered out the window.

"Are you sure he's coming?" The lone waitress, hands on her hips, joined Eleanor and scanned the parking lot. "You can sit at a table if you want to."

"No, thanks. He'll be here soon."

"If you say so. You can seat yourselves whenever you're ready. Menus are on the table." She sashayed toward the kitchen, and Eleanor resumed her watch.

How did wives and mothers do it... worry and wait for their children to get home, when something didn't feel right? Even little things, like this, when you knew it was really all right, but you just had to see for yourself?

Fifteen minutes, not ten. Eleanor ran into the parking lot to meet him as he stepped out of the black SUV. "Are you okay?"

"Hi! I'm fine. It wasn't a big collision."

Eleanor examined the front end of the truck. No broken glass. The parking lot lights reflected from the shiny paint and smooth chrome. She looked at David, who'd followed her. "I don't see a dent."

"Keep going." He walked around the SUV. "It's on this side. I hope I don't have to replace the whole door."

"The door? The back door? How did you do that?"

"I didn't do anything," David said. "I was driving along, minding my own business, and this dumb deer ran out and threw herself at my truck. Just ran right into it."

"No way. You were driving in a straight line and it ran into you from the side?" Eleanor asked, incredulous. "What happened to the deer?"

"I think she heard me calling the sheriff's office, asking them to come out and kill her, and she got up and ran away."

"Asking them to kill her?"

"She was lying in the middle of the road, but she was still alive," David said. "I didn't want to leave her suffering."

"Oh." That made sense, but it sounded horrible. She

couldn't imagine having to kill an animal you'd just hit with your car. "I suppose she was just stunned." Eleanor looked at the dent. Did deer get concussions? "I hope she's okay."

"She ran off just fine once she woke up. I wouldn't have left if I thought she was really injured."

What a nice guy. Eleanor nodded toward the restaurant door. "Should we go in? It's cold out here."

He glanced at the flickering "open" sign in the window. "Do you come here often?"

"Never been here before. I found it in the yellow pages."

He raised his brows. "The yellow pages? As in, a real phone book?"

"Yep. There was a phone book on the shelf in the office, and it seemed easier than searching online." She bit her lip. "It is kind of a dive. I don't know my way around here yet."

"Well, I saw a Subway and a Dairy Queen on the way into town, but I'd rather have a hot meal. I'm sure this is fine." He opened the door. "After you."

"He showed up!" The waitress's voice was loud enough to catch the attention of everyone in the restaurant. "You folks sit wherever you want. I'll be right there."

"Sorry," Eleanor said. "Next time, we can find something in St. Cloud." Would there be a next time?

"Larry said there's a good place on 169 north of town—Rough Cut. He says it doesn't look like much from the outside, but it's got the best food in town."

"I go by there every day! I thought it was mostly just a bar and liquor store." Eleanor sipped her water. "I live a few miles north of there."

"North? You really do have a long commute."

"It's a pretty drive, though. I'll have the Milaca Burger without cheese, with the chicken dumpling soup instead of fries, please." Eleanor handed her menu to the waitress, who tossed it on the next table.

"That sounds good to me," David said, "but I'll have the cheese on mine, and fries, too."

"Soup and fries?" The waitress accepted his menu and put it with the others. "Both? Are you sure?"

"Right now, I could eat a horse."

If he'd smiled at Eleanor like that, she'd have melted into a gooey puddle. The waitress just rolled her eyes and walked away.

"I wish they'd pay waitstaff a regular wage," Eleanor said. "They could just add it into the price of the food. Then a tip would mean something instead of being an obligation."

"And the absence of a tip would mean that you got bad service, instead of meaning that you're a jerk."

"Exactly!" She beamed at him. "As the system works now, the tip reflects the quality of the customer instead of the quality of the service."

"Huh." David nodded. "You're right. I hadn't heard it put that way before. I always try to extend grace and maybe give a little more when the service is bad. I fold it up inside a tract."

A tract? She kept forgetting he was in school to be a pastor. They'd spent most of their last conversation talking about her, as he peeled away her half-truths and evasions. It was his turn.

"Have you always lived around here?"

"Yes. I grew up in Mora. It's only about an hour away, so I can go home pretty often, to see my family.

"Mora's that little Swedish town, right?" Eleanor

asked. "The one with the big Dala horse?"

"That's the one."

"Are you Swedish?" He didn't have the classic icy blue eyes of the Andersons and Nielsons. His were warm. Hazel eyes, brown and green and gold. Warm, with dark brown lashes and eyebrows.

"...grandpa. I think we're mostly northern European, but not all Scandinavian."

With a start, Eleanor brought her attention back to the conversation.

"I've never thought of myself as specifically Swedish... just American. Aunt Violet is all about our heritage and family tree, but Mom and Dad aren't interested in that kind of thing. They're pretty proud of being Minnesotan, though." She stretched the third syllable, and he laughed.

"Minnesota nice?" He suggested.

"They made up that term to describe my parents," Eleanor said. "They epitomize Minnesota nice. They make Canadians look rude."

He really did have a nice smile. When his lips turned up like that, he had little parentheses curling around the corners and just a hint of a dimple in his left cheek. What on earth was he doing with the matchmaking agency? There must be something wrong with him... something she just hadn't seen yet.

"Here you go." The waitress set a large tray on the next table and began unloading it. "Two Milaca Burgers, two bowls of soup, and one order of fries. You want anything else?"

No, Eleanor wouldn't need anything else to eat for three days. The hamburger had four patties, separated by ruffly lettuce and thick slices of tomato and onion. Bacon strips protruded from the top and bottom. No toothpick would have held it together; the cook had stabbed a knife through the top bun.

"Wow. How big is this thing?" David gazed at his burger, apparently awestruck. His had cheese between each patty, too, just melted enough to ooze off the edges. He pulled out the knife and set it on his plate, not taking his eyes off the hamburger.

"A pound. It was on the menu. Didn't you read it?" The waitress picked up one of their discarded menus and flipped it open. "Four quarter pound patties. You do the math; it adds up to one pound." She snapped the menu shut. "Anything else?"

Eleanor shook her head. "I think we're good."

"Thank you," David said. "It looks great."

Oh right. He was going to be a pastor. He had to be nice. She pulled a fry from the basket and held it up. "This is the biggest french fry I have ever seen."

"There must be four whole potatoes here. You'll have to share them with me." He pushed the basket toward her."

"Are you kidding? They must super-size everything. Look at this soup!" She picked up her spoon and dipped it in the bowl—the tureen—of chicken dumpling soup. "I hope they have take-home containers."

"Would you mind if I say grace?"

Eleanor let go of her spoon, and it slid to the bottom of her bowl. So much for impressing him with good table manners. She used her fork to fish it out. "Sure. That would be nice."

She hesitated, uncertain of the protocol, but he started without ceremony. She caught up quickly—chin tucked into her chest, eyes closed, and hands clasped like a child's, on the edge of the table.

"Oh, Lord our God, how great you are."

Eleanor's eyes flew open. She hadn't expected such... volume. David looked relaxed. At least his eyes were closed, so he hadn't seen her reaction. She closed her own again, squeezing them shut, hoping he prayed fast. What was wrong with "Come, Lord Jesus"? She knew that one.

"Thank you, God, for this food, an abundant provision for us. You are so good to us. Thank you for this time Eleanor and I can spend together, getting to know each other."

What was he doing? Eleanor peeked at him. He still looked calm. Comfortable.

"We know that your hand is on this situation, Lord, and you knew that we would meet like this. It's a part of your plan, and our heart's desire is to live out that plan according to your will and glorify you. Help us to see what your will is, God. Show us what we should do and help us stay on that path. Be close to us and guide us, moment by moment, every step of the way, into the relationship you want us to have."

Why was he talking about this now, out loud, praying in front of everyone in the restaurant? She rubbed her fingers, numb from being clenched so tightly.

"Be with us this evening, God. Help us to keep the words of our mouth and the meditations of our hearts clean and acceptable in your sight, Oh Lord, our rock and our redeemer. In the name of Jesus, we pray, Amen."

"Amen." She untangled her fingers and flexed her hands under the table. How was she supposed to respond to that?

"Here. Take my spoon." He reached across the table

and set it down. "I'll get another one after I finish this amazing hamburger." He turned the plate, admiring it from every angle. "I feel like I should take a picture and post it on Instagram."

"You use Instagram?" Eleanor laughed. "Really?"

"No, but my sister and cousins do. At our family meals, they're allowed to have their phones out long enough to take pictures of the food and post them on Instagram."

"Every meal?"

"It seems like it. I don't know how it started, but now it's a bona fide Reid family tradition—at least for the girls. The guys just want to eat."

"Oh, my goodness -" Eleanor broke off. "I'm sorry, I didn't mean to interrupt you, but this soup is delicious. The dumplings are perfect, and look!" She scooped up a spoonful of soup. "It has real chicken and carrots in it. They must have made it from scratch. Get a spoon and try it."

"Not yet." David handed her a french fry. "These are great." She watched him, enjoying his happiness. Her mother would have pursed her lips and looked away as he made happy, appreciative noises as he chewed. Good manners meant ignoring other people's bad manners. Eleanor liked it.

David wiped his mouth with the paper napkin. "This burger is incredible. How's yours?"

She set down her soup spoon, carefully, and bit into the burger. Perfect. She swallowed and wiped sauce from her chin before opening her mouth to comment.

David didn't wait for her response. He waved both arms in the air. "Hey, Susan!"

The waitress's name was Susan? Eleanor remembered a name tag, but she hadn't read it.

"What do you need?" The waitress approached, surveying their table. She frowned at David. "Something wrong with your soup?"

"I took his spoon," Eleanor said. "He needs a new one. The soup is delicious. I love chicken and dumpling soup, and this is the best I've ever had. Ever."

The waitress lit up, transformed by a broad smile. "Thanks! It's my dad's recipe. I usually just chop things, but he let me make the dumplings this time. I can't wait to tell him!"

"The burger is awesome. The fries, too." David took another one. "Do you make them, too?"

She shook her head, laughing. "I'm nearly forty years old, and Dad still won't let me near the grill or fryer. People do like my pies, though. I'll get you a spoon."

Eleanor stared after her. David returned to his burger.

"That was really nice of you."

"What was?" David raised his eyebrows. "Complimenting her on the food? It's true."

"It... it made her so happy."

"It's true," he repeated. "'Pleasant words are a honeycomb, Sweet to the soul and healing to the bones.' Another version says, 'Kind words are like honey—they cheer you up and make you feel strong.'"

"It did cheer her up." Bible verses and praying. She didn't really mind the praying. She just hadn't been expecting it. Otherwise, he was easy to be around. She liked him.

Eleanor set her hamburger on the plate. She wasn't here for a relationship. David was kind, open, friendly, caring enough to stay with an injured deer—and in search of a real relationship. A wife. Instead, he got a selfish woman who only wanted a temporary fix. God hadn't made their match. This wasn't His plan. It was Eleanor's plan. She was using him.

"I had a good time tonight. Thanks." David glanced at his truck. "At least, dinner was good. I'm glad we didn't go to Dairy Queen or Subway."

Eleanor held up her stack of Styrofoam boxes. "I'll be eating leftovers for a while. I can't believe you actually finished yours and ate the pie, too."

"I didn't have much choice, when she gave it to us for free, and it was excellent pie."

She couldn't see his face in the shadows, but she heard the smile in his voice.

"You know," he said, "we really should talk about this Betwixt Two Hearts business."

Yes, they should. "Would you like to have lunch together one day this week?"

"That would be great. How about tomorrow?"

She chuckled. "How about Friday? Uncle Gary has me booked solid for the next two days. I'm getting a crash course in mechanical contracting."

"We'll have a lot in common. I can imagine it, and you can make it happen! A match made in heaven."

No, it wasn't.

14

Eleanor wiped sweaty palms on her jeans and breathed deeply, trying to get air into her depleted lungs. She couldn't do anything about the drumming in her chest, but she had to remember to breathe steadily.

She scooted forward in the chair, positioned the fabric under the presser foot, and carefully lowered the foot. The fabric slid away. She caught it before it fell to the floor this time. Wordlessly, Aunt Violet handed her another pair of perfectly aligned strips.

"Are you sure I shouldn't pin it? Just one or two pins? Even if I can get them started, I'm afraid they're going to slip apart while I'm sewing."

The older woman leaned over her. "Your left hand goes here, holding these threads." She hooked the threads and laid them across Eleanor's fingers. "Hold on to those, but don't pull too hard. You just want to get the seam started smoothly and not get the threads tangled underneath. Once it's going, you'll use your left hand to hold the strips loosely together here and your right hand to steer them through the machine."

"And I just sew the whole thing without stopping? The whole strip?" Impossible.

"When you get to the end of the first pair of strips,"

Violet said, "you'll start the next one without breaking your threads. I'll help you when you get there."

"Okay." Eleanor tried to position her hands, but it felt like she had too many of them—or not enough.

"Stop."

She lifted her foot from the pedal and looked at her aunt. "What did I do wrong?"

"You're getting off your quarter inch."

Eleanor looked at the fabric. She'd practiced on scrap fabric, but maintaining a straight seam allowance was harder on the real thing. "Okay," she repeated. "Should I take it out or can I just sew over it?"

"Sew over it. Start from the beginning."

Great. She'd sewn six inches and had to start over. The cutting had been bad enough, especially after Penny took her aside and said that under no circumstances should she leave Aunt Violet alone with a rotary cutter. Apparently, Violet did just fine with cutting as long as she had good lighting, wasn't tired, took frequent breaks and had someone nearby to apply tourniquets if necessary.

"Stop now."

She only had an inch left. Eleanor slumped back in the chair. "Did I mess it up?"

"You're doing fine. You need to start a new set now. Just like this." Aunt Violet set another pair of strips behind the ones she just sewn. "You're chain-piecing, one piece after another, without cutting the threads in between, so you'll end up with one long chain of them. Just keep going."

"Got it." Eleanor embarked on the second set of strips. As soon as the first was clear, Aunt Violet cut the threads between them.

Eleanor stopped. "Why did you cut them?"

"I'm going to press while you sew. If you were alone, you'd just keep going and press when you were done with that sewing step." Violet carried the strips to the ironing board and spoke over her shoulder. "Keep going."

I HATE QUILTING.

Eleanor typed out the text and deleted it. Brittany wouldn't understand unless she went into detail, and it wasn't nearly as scary in the telling as it had been in the doing. Besides, Brittany was probably tired of hearing about the perils of Eleanor.

She flopped back against the stack of pillows. How could quilting be so exhausting? Maybe it wasn't, once you got used to it, or if you didn't have such an exacting teacher, but this was definitely not a relaxing hobby. She'd never finish before the anniversary party. Maybe she should have taken out a loan to buy her parents a new car.

Or perhaps she should just pray harder for a blizzard. Maybe if she could pray like David did, God would answer her prayers. He didn't, usually, or maybe she just didn't usually pray. She didn't even think about God, most of the time, so how could she go running to him when she had a problem? You couldn't just ignore people for months at a time and then start asking for favors.

"Dear God, I really don't want to go to this party alone, but I will, if you want me to." She thought about mentioning the blizzard and decided not to. "I don't want to hurt David, but I don't want to lose him, either. Or rather, lose the chance to get to know him, or something like that. Mostly, I don't want to hurt him. In Jesus' name,

Amen."

Nothing happened. She rolled over, burying her face in the pillows. She couldn't just rush right in and tell him she'd only joined the agency to get one date. She didn't want him to despise her.

"Well, here we are again." Eleanor smiled as she slid into the booth opposite David. "I meant to ask you. Have you heard from that matchmaking agency at all? Are we supposed to report in or anything? I didn't know if there was any kind of follow-up."

Her vivid eyes reflected the blue sky and white snow outside the window. Not denim today—she was pure Scandinavian. David brought his attention back to her question. "Not that I know of. It sounds like it's up to us to initiate contact if we have questions or want a new match or to cancel."

"A new match?" Eleanor raised her brows. "You know, this is a lot more awkward than I thought it would be. I thought meeting a stranger would be the awkward part, but this 'what now?' stage is worse. I mean, what if one of us didn't like the other person?"

"Or what if you wanted to date a few different guys before making a commitment to the first one?" asked David. "Or what if you had different objectives in signing up for the service in the first place?" If their relationship was going to end, he'd rather have it happen now than later.

"Right." She toyed with her straw. "Why did you sign up for it, David?"

That was blunt. David suddenly wished he hadn't brought it up. He'd tried to formulate this explanation, muttering under his breath as he practiced it, but there didn't seem to be any easy way to explain he didn't want to keep looking for a woman who might not show up—and then have a long courtship and engagement before getting married and having a bunch of kids.

Eleanor sat, watching his face.

"What about you?" He asked. "What made you decide to sign up?" Her gaze dropped to her hands, and he went on. "Are you looking for an exclusive relationship? A long-term relationship?" He took a deep breath and used the M word. "The goal of the agency is traditional marriage. That's what I want."

At her continued silence, he pressed. "Is that why you signed up?"

She hunched her shoulders in a shrug and then relaxed. Instead of answering, she repeated, "But why the agency? Why not a nice girl from your church or a friend of a friend?"

"You're a good volleyball player." She looked up, startled, and he continued. "You keep throwing the ball back into my court."

She smiled. "My next question was going to be about the church. How do they feel about internet dating?"

"That would be spiking the ball." David smiled back at her. "I don't know. I didn't ask. I prayed about it, though, and I think it's a fine thing to do. Some people might object to it, I guess, but it's becoming pretty mainstream. The difference with Betwixt is that it's not a dating website. It's a matchmaking service."

"But why use the agency instead of finding someone local? Waiting for God to send the right woman?"

Eleanor's persistence and his conscience forced him into the truth. "I'm nearly thirty years old. When my parents were this age, they'd already had all their kids. Now, in their early 50's they're enjoying life without us. They should have grandchildren while they're still young enough to enjoy them."

"You're worried that your parents will be too old to enjoy your children?"

He sounded like an idiot. "No, I'm worried that I will be too old to enjoy mine."

She shook her head as if to clear it. "You... Are you saying that you think you're getting old and you want to get married and have children right away, before you get too old to enjoy them? So, they'll grow up and leave home, so you can have an empty nest and then grandchildren right away after that?"

"Um..."

"That requires the cooperation of a lot of people, David, starting with your wife and then your children and their spouses—all so you can dandle grandchildren on your still-functional knee?"

Was she outraged or laughing at him? He couldn't tell. David opened his mouth, hoping something good would come out.

"A hundred years ago, you could have sent for a mail-order bride."

Definitely laughter. He felt the heat in his face and knew he was turning red.

Eleanor sobered and reached across the table to touch his hand. "I'm sorry. I shouldn't tease you. You're doing exactly what the website offered. Exactly."

He relaxed his grip on the water glass. "That's what I said, when Larry showed me the ad: mail-order brides.

He reminded me that Abraham sent his servants out to bring back a wife for his son. Not exactly the same thing, but similar." David grinned. "My mom has a bookcase full of historical romance, and I'm pretty sure there are some mail-order bride books in there."

"I wonder what she'd think if she knew you sent for a mail-order bride," Eleanor took a sip of her water. "Personally, I think it's a practical idea."

"Personally, you sent for a mail-order husband." David looked at her. "Or why did you sign up?"

She set down her cup. "I wanted a date for Valentine's Day."

He waited, but she didn't continue. "And?"

Silent, she picked at her cuticles, glancing at him from under her lashes.

"A date for Valentine's Day?" David asked, incredulous. Eleanor had signed up for a matchmaking agency for just one date? "That's all? Just a date for Valentine's Day? Why?" His voice was too loud. Angry. "That's... I'm sure you could get a date for one night without having to sign up for a matchmaking agency!" He stopped and moderated his tone. "I feel like that's deceptive." He felt hurt and angry and humiliated, too. "Betwixt Two Hearts isn't an escort service."

"Yeah." The word was a sigh. "I realized that the first time we talked, at the hospital. Then, at dinner, I just... it was nice. Fun. I shouldn't have signed up." She kept her gaze on her hands. "I didn't know what else to do."

"Why?" he asked again. How could a girl like Eleanor be that desperate for a Valentine's Day date? Had he completely misjudged her?

She rubbed her eyebrows with her fingertips, covering her face. "It's in Minneapolis. An anniversary party for my parents, and they're expecting me to bring a date. I didn't want to go without a date." She lowered her hands and finally looked at him. Clouds had drifted over the sun, and her eyes were denim again, and worried. "I've already decided to go alone. I wasn't going to ask you. It was a stupid idea."

"Yeah, it was." David heard the roughness in his voice. He hadn't expected her to be looking for an instant husband, but she should have been looking for a relationship, at least, open to romance. That's what the agency was for.

She slumped. "I am sorry." Eleanor pulled her purse onto her lap and dug through it. She laid a twenty-dollar bill next to her plate, smoothing it carefully, not meeting his eyes. "I'm truly sorry, David. You're a really nice guy and I hope you find a wonderful wife."

He watched her pull on her coat as she walked out the door. He wanted to say something, but not the wrong thing, so he said nothing.

15

"Hey, Sis! How are things going up there in the frozen tundra?"

"Hi, Soren." Eleanor tapped the speaker button and handed the phone to Aunt Violet. "I'm putting you on speaker, because I'm driving. Is everyone okay there?" She couldn't remember the last time she'd talked to Soren on the phone.

"Everyone's good. Missing you. When are you coming back to civilization?"

"I'll be there for the anniversary party! I'm looking forward to it." That wasn't what he meant, of course.

"I called to let you know there's a professional development workshop coming up on Saturday, in Minnetonka. I'm not sure of all the details, but you'll be able to pick up some of the clock hours you need in mental illness, suicide prevention and positive behavioral intervention. I'll email you the link. It's sponsored by Westerfield, so you'd be able to meet some of the administration there."

Eleanor rolled her eyes. "Golly, Soren, that sounds like a lot of fun, but I don't think I'll be able to make it."

Aunt Violet snorted.

"I'll send you the link. I know you have a couple years before renewal, but it would be a good opportunity to make some connections."

"I'm going to be busy all day Saturday," Eleanor said. "Soren, we just arrived at church, so I'm going to hang up now."

"Who's with you?"

"Aunt Violet. You're on speaker phone. Say hello, Aunt Violet." Eleanor grinned, wishing they had time for a nice long discussion of family history. It would serve him right.

"Hello, Aunt Violet! How are you?"

"I'm very good, Soren. How are you?"

"Never better. I hope you ladies have a good Sunday. Eleanor, don't forget the workshop. You can sign up at the door, but it's best to register ahead of time."

"I'm not going, Soren."

"Just think about it, Ellie. Talk to you later. Bye!"

Had Aunt Violet told the pastor what to say? A spurt of outrage subsided when she remembered that her aunt didn't know about Betwixt. The whole message was obviously aimed specifically at her, though.

She wasn't arrogant—not proud, like the pastor said. She knew she didn't always do the right thing, but she tried. She was an honest person, except for little white lies like telling Soren she wasn't available on Saturday or telling Brittany her new sweater was pretty. Or shading the truth on that matchmaking agency application, trying to game the algorithm. It had worked. She got exactly the kind of man she wanted.

But the Lord weighs the heart. Not only had it been

bad because it hurt David, it was wrong because God saw her heart and knew her intentions. She was so self-centered that she hadn't considered how her actions would affect the man she was matched with...

"A person may think their own ways are right, but the Lord weighs the heart." The pastor leaned over the pulpit. "Let's say you've done something. Something kind of bad... it doesn't have to be terribly wicked. You failed to send your mother a birthday gift. On the day of her birthday, you only remember because you see it on Facebook!"

A ripple of amusement stirred the congregation. He continued. "At this point, you should probably post a birthday greeting on Facebook, preferably one of those long messages about having the best mother in the world. That's a good starting point. You can call her. You can call a florist and have flowers delivered. Probably, you're coming up with some good excuses for the lack of a present. You had to work late and couldn't get to the store. You're low on cash. You didn't know what she wanted. She always tells you not to get her anything, anyhow.

"But where was your heart? You just plain forgot, maybe because you didn't care enough to put it in your phone. Or, if you thought about it earlier in the week, it never became a priority. Maybe you were saving your money for a new television. Maybe you're mad because she did something you didn't like. God sees your heart. He weighs it. He knows the truth—and your mom probably does, too."

The pastor chuckled. "That's a pretty silly analogy, but I think you can see what I mean. A person may think their own ways are right. Those excuses you came up with? They weren't only for her. You were busy justifying your behavior. Coming up with rational reasons for your actions. But the Lord wasn't interested in your excuses. He's weighing your heart. Very few of us have pure hearts. The heart is deceitful and desperately wicked. Who can know it? God can. He knows your heart.

Eleanor gathered up her belongings as soon as the last song ended, smiling brightly at Aunt Violet. "I'm going to use the bathroom, and then I'll bring the car around front."

"No hurry, Dear. I'm going to talk to Constance for a few minutes."

How could that pastor make assumptions about her motivations? He didn't even know her. She shook her head, suddenly aware of the absurdity of her attitude. If anyone had told the pastor what to say, it must have been God. Had she thought her own way was right when she filled out that application? Yes, it made sense to her. Had her heart been pure? No. And God knew.

But it was pretty hypocritical of the pastor to say doing the right thing was more acceptable than sacrifice just before he passed the offering plate.

"How are you ladies doing?"

Uncle Carl reminded her of his brother—cheerful, energetic, and kind. Eleanor wished she'd known them better, earlier in life. She liked it here.

"We're good," Violet said. "I was just telling Constance that we're not going to the nursing home today. Olof's getting a lot of company today, and I didn't sleep well last night. I'm going to treat myself to a Sunday afternoon nap."

"Good idea." Carl turned to his wife. "Can I do that?"

"Certainly, right after we get home from seeing Uncle Olof."

Carl turned to Eleanor. "Gary tells me you're keeping the business afloat while he's in there."

"I'm trying. He's very patient with me."

"He says you're doing great." He clapped her on the shoulder and looked at his wife. "Every time I go there, he complains about Cheryl. He says she's abusing him."

Constance chuckled. "Physical therapy is hard work. I'm glad she's back. We should have her over for dinner one night soon."

"Larry!" David hurried across the parking lot. "Are you going to be at the Y for basketball this afternoon?"

"I wasn't planning on it. Did you need me?"

"I'd be grateful if you'd come." David said. "There's a boy there... I'm a little worried about him, and I don't have time to talk to him while I'm coaching. I was hoping you could come by and chat with him."

Larry shook his head. "I should just set up one of those booths like Lucy had in the Peanuts cartoons. 'Psychiatric help. Five cents.'"

"I've got five cents." David made a show of digging in his pockets. "Maybe even a dollar. Most of those guys could use a listening ear. I thought the basketball would be a good outreach, and I'd be able to help the kids, maybe draw them in to some of the youth activities at church, but now I'm running the program and don't even have time to talk to the boys."

Larry looked at his watch. "How could I resist that appeal? Sure, I'll be there. But if you want to help them, get yourself some volunteers to help with the coaching, so you can have more one-on-one time with the kids."

"Thanks, Larry." David hesitated. "You know, I haven't seen Angela at work in the last few days. Do you know if she's okay? I thought I'd ask you before asking Cal."

"You should ask Cal."

That was interesting. David nodded. It might mean that Angela had become a client, or Angela might be in trouble, or maybe Larry just didn't want to gossip. Maybe he just didn't know. David hoped she was okay.

16

E ncore, encore!"
Eleanor grinned. It was a sing-along, not a performance. They just wanted to keep singing. She looked at Gary. "Do we do encores?

"It's up to you, kiddo."

She leafed through her songbook. "How about 'Michael, Row Your Boat Ashore' and then 'Take Me Out to the Ballgame'? I know those pretty well."

"Sounds good. We'll get everyone good and riled up before lunch."

Uncle Gary didn't believe in paperless offices. Right now, his office was a tiny bedroom in a nursing home — a rehabilitation center. In addition to his tablet and laptop, he had a printer/fax machine, a portable scanner, and a wastebasket. A dry erase board leaned against the window, and a small file cabinet had replaced the original bedside table.

"Did you bring me that phone book?"

Eleanor pulled it from her bag. "I did, and the portfolio, too."

"Thanks. Set the phone book over there by the catalogs and bring me the portfolio."

"You know, Uncle Gary, you never used half this stuff when you were in the office." She picked up a pad of sticky notes. "I've never seen you use a sticky note. I don't know why you wanted a calculator, either; you always use the one on your phone or computer."

He peered over his glasses at her. "You young people are so disrespectful. I might need it, and I can't be calling you in the middle of the night to bring me a sticky note."

"In case you need a sticky note in the middle of the night?"

"Be prepared." He closed the portfolio and held it on his lap. "Would you be willing to take this out to a job site for me? The guy's only going to be in town on Friday, and I want him to see these projects I've been doing with Ridgewell. You met David Reid in the hospital."

"He came to help us when you had your accident, remember? I've met him a few times, now."

"Really! He seems like a good guy. So, the man at the job site is John Frans. I'll give him a call to tell him you're coming."

Ten minutes later, Eleanor hitched her computer bag over her shoulder and accepted the portfolio from her uncle. "Do I need a hard hat at the job site?"

"Yes, you do. I've got a few of them around. Maybe we should just order you one of your own."

She'd like a hard hat of her own. Pink would be silly; maybe a light blue.

Gary spoke as she stopped in the doorway. "You're doing a great job here, Ellie. If you're still here by summer and want to stick it out, I've got a permanent place for you.

It's like this—mostly take-offs in the winter and office work in the summer, but if we start getting more of the Ridgewell projects, or things like that, we'll be working with new materials and suppliers. More crew. It would pay a little more than what you're getting now." He grinned. "Nothing like you'd make as a teacher, and the benefits aren't that good, but think about it. I'd be glad to have you.

Eleanor hummed as she rounded the corner of the house and let herself into the annex, pretending she was the 10-year-old Kathy, returning to this big crowded house after school every day. Instead of Aunt Violet, Grandma would have been here, ready to greet her children with cookies and milk.

Actually, Grandma was probably busy sewing when they got home, just like Aunt Violet was doing now. Eleanor found her in the quilting room, removing Karl's quilt from the frame.

"Is it all done?"

Violet nodded without speaking. She folded the quilt and carried it across the hall to the sewing room. Eleanor hesitated. Did Violet want to be left alone, or did she want company. It would be better to have company when you wanted to be alone—after all, you could send people away—than to be alone when you wanted to have someone there with you.

Her phone rang. Eleanor sighed. Having reached such a philosophical conclusion, she couldn't send her mother to voice mail.

"Hello, Mom!"

"Hi, there. How are you? I haven't talked to you in a while."

"Oh, busy. Gary's still laid up. He's supposed to be there for at least another four weeks, so we're running everything from two locations. I'm glad he's able to do his rehab in Milaca instead of St. Cloud." Eleanor poured herself a glass of water and sniffed at the beef stew Aunt Violet had made for dinner. "The nursing home is between here and the office."

"That's nice," Kathy said. "I was calling to let you know that Westerfield is hosting a Professional Development workshop. It's on Saturday, and it looks good. I thought we could go together."

"Soren told me about that. I'm not planning on going, Mom."

"You're going to need the clock hours for re-licensure. This would be a good place to get some of them."

Eleanor sat and propped her elbows on the table. "Mom, I still have two years on my license. If I decide to renew it, I have plenty of time to get the credits I need."

"You don't want to wait until the last minute," her mother warned her. "Look it up online. I'll send you the link."

"Are you sure we're going to finish this in time?" Eleanor rose and stretched. It should have been a comfortable chair, but she sat with every muscle tensed, hunched ten inches from the sewing machine, not blinking as she sewed. "We haven't finished a single block yet, and we only have three weeks left. I wish I had more time to work on it."

At the nursing home, Gary made lists and scheduled her day, and she was still busy at the office, keeping track of everything. One of his crew had quit, and the staff at the nursing home had flatly refused to let him do job interviews in their conference room.

Here at home, she worked on the quilt under the gimlet eye of Aunt Violet and tried not to think about her wretched treatment of David.

"We'll finish it on Saturday," Violet said, "so you'll be busy all day Saturday. Hand me those scissors, will you please?"

Busy all day Saturday. Eleanor handed the scissors to her aunt. Violet didn't meet her eyes.

"This old rayon doesn't hold up very well. The armholes are already frayed." Violet laid the pink dress across the cutting table.

Was she really going to cut that up? Eleanor started to object and then fell silent. If Marlys didn't want it, who would?

"That was Molly's wedding dress?"

"Yes." Violet's terse response didn't invite further comment. "You need to press those outward now."

Eleanor complied, watching her aunt while she waited for the iron to get hot. It would be natural for an elderly, unmarried woman to care about her extended family. Her nieces and nephews were the closest thing she had to children of her own. She'd even lived with them from the time they were born.

"Marlys sent all sorts of things in that box," Violet said. "Some of it must have come from her mother's family. I think she was just downsizing and unloaded it all on me."

She was probably the only one who would take it.

Eleanor walked over to the table. The limp fabric didn't look like a wedding dress. If she hadn't seen the photograph, she wouldn't have been able to imagine it as a dress at all.

"She must have been tiny."

Violet nodded. "She was, but she was a spitfire. She could hold her own with Axel. I always felt sorry for her students."

"She was a teacher?"

"For nearly fifty years," Violet said, "until they sold the feed mill and moved to Florida."

"Three years was enough for me. Was she a mentor for my mother, too, like Maybel Furster?"

"Oh, no. Molly wasn't a mentor to anyone, and she was especially strict with your mom and the others. Maria tried to get them reassigned, but there was only one classroom for each grade level. Of course, it was probably hard on Molly, to have her twelve-year-old nephews in her classroom, too." A fond smile curved Violet's lips. "Those boys were mischievous."

"Gary and Carl? I bet they were."

"And Scott," Violet said. "Colleen could be a handful, too, but your mom was always well-behaved. Is that your phone?"

"It's Laurie. She can leave a message."

Aunt Violet raised her brows. "You can take a break to talk to her, if you want to."

"I don't. I know exactly what she's calling for. The same thing Mom and Soren called about—a continuing education workshop there in the cities. I'm not going."

"I see. The iron should be hot now."

Eleanor obediently returned to the ironing board. "What else was in the box? Did you get the pictures?"

"Yes, but I had most of them already. There were some letters and a notebook that belonged to Kristina, but I set those aside for now. Then she sent some other things that couldn't have belonged to us: a packet of postcards, a little wooden box with cigarettes in it, a pocket watch and a locket with an old picture of a man and woman. No one I know. There were some other things, too, that might have been Axel's after he moved to Florida."

"But you don't think the postcards and cigarettes were? And the pocket watch?" Eleanor used the side of the iron to push open the triangles. The pink and gray fabrics were perfect for her mother.

"No. They look older—from the 40's, maybe, and I think the inscription on the pocket watch is German. The postcards have churches and towns that look German, too."

"Maybe they're souvenirs of the war," Eleanor said. "Soldiers brought home all sorts of stuff after both world wars, didn't they?"

"Not our soldiers."

Eleanor shut her eyes. That was probably the single most insensitive comment she'd made in her entire life.

Violet went on before she could think of a way to apologize. "Axel was very prejudiced against Germans. He would have burned these things, not saved them." She sighed. "The war was hard on Axel. He was just 13 when Hans and Karl died. His big brothers. All his life, he wouldn't even be polite if he thought someone might be German. He wouldn't shake their hand or wait on them at the feed mill. No, these things belonged to someone else."

Eleanor tipped the hard hat onto her head, wishing she'd tried it on before she left the office. It still didn't fit. No matter how she adjusted the straps, it still perched on top of her head, making her feel like one of those bobblehead dolls her brother had on a shelf in his library. With a scowl at her reflection in the rear-view mirror, she jammed the hard hat down as far as it would go and opened the car door.

She'd had trouble deciding what to wear, but jeans and plaid flannel seemed a safe choice. Eleanor looked at her feet doubtfully, hoping tennis shoes were adequate. She didn't own any steel-toe boots. She wasn't staying long, but as a representative of Evergreen Services, she wanted to make a good impression on Mr. Frans.

"Hey, lady. You can't park there."

Why not? There weren't any signs, and the small lot already held half a dozen trucks. He should have been clued in by the hard hat; she was there on official business. "I'm looking for John Frans."

The man shook his head. "No one here by that name. This is private property."

"I'm looking for a job site next to the old schoolhouse." Eleanor looked at the assortment of construction equipment. Now what?

"Is that the one you're looking for?"

She followed his pointing finger. Four men, two of them in suits, and one lone backhoe. The ground wasn't even broken yet. Suits.

Oh, God, please, no. She'd been sending up more of these silent prayers lately, usually in the office, when she was stressed. She hadn't felt any response, but at least she hadn't had a full-blown anxiety attack.

And she wasn't going to have one now. "I'll only be here about ten minutes. Can I leave my car that long?"

"The boss'll be back from lunch in half an hour. He'll want to park there."

"I'll be gone by then. Thank you."

Clutching the portfolio, she walked across the frozen ground with her most confident stride. One of the men raised a hand in greeting, and as she responded, she realized she still wore the yellow hard hat. She sent another panicked prayer heavenward. It was becoming a habit.

She pasted a bright smile on her face as she neared them, but it dimmed when she recognized the man on the end. David's smile looked a little forced, too. She'd never seen him in a suit before. He looked amazing, and she looked like a slob. A slob in a hard hat and tennis shoes. She smiled harder.

"You must be Eleanor. Gary told us you'd be coming. I'm John Frans, and these are my partners, Jake and Luke Brown." The tallest man reached out to shake her hand. "David was telling us you've worked with Ridgewell before."

Eleanor nodded. The hard hat slipped over her eyes. She pushed it back, and it tumbled to the ground behind her. She was putting on a comedy act, not impressing them with her professionalism.

David retrieved the hard hat and turned it over, examining the interior. Maybe he'd fix it for her. She handed the portfolio to John and gestured toward the larger construction site. "Gary said the job site was next to the old schoolhouse. I thought it was that one. Are you just getting started here?"

"Just checking out Ridgewell's proposal so far. We got sidetracked by the POW camp." He gestured toward the row of cabins at the wood line. "I never knew this was out here."

"I never knew we had POW camps in Minnesota," one of the other men said.

"Fifteen of them," Eleanor said. She'd taught her middle-school students about it, for three years in a row. She found it fascinating; they just wanted to know if the prisoners were tortured. "They came as agricultural workers, because the men were gone to war."

"Slave labor camps!" The comment came from the third man. "Were they tortured?"

"Didn't the locals object to having the enemy there?"

"No, not tortured. They were treated in strict accordance with the Geneva Convention, which meant that they had better housing and food than many of the local people did, during the war. People did object to that." She needed to leave before the sight of her car being towed away put a cap on her less-than-stellar performance. "You can look it up online. It's very interesting. It was nice meeting you."

She shook hands with each of the men, ending with David, who returned her hard hat. She wasn't prepared for the warm smile that accompanied it, or the sympathy in his hazel eyes. If he was going to be a pastor, though, he'd have to forgive people, right? And feel sorry for them when they made fools of themselves.

Worry replaced depressing thoughts of David as she drove into the office parking lot. Some of the crew, even more dirty than usual, lounged outside the office, smoking or talking on their phones. The crew supervisor, Tim, stood with his back to her. She closed her eyes and sent up another prayer. Soon, she'd have to make time to say more than "help me" when she talked to God.

She gathered her tote bag and Gary's books, plonked the hard hat on her head, and pushed the car door open with her foot. The hat fit.

"Ellie." Tim came toward her, followed by several of his men.

She gasped. "What happened?" The odor made her eyes water. Resisting the temptation to close the door and roll up the window, she stepped out of the car and surveyed them. They looked like they'd climbed through a fireplace, with ashes and soot, and then rolled in... a bean bag chair. "Is that insulation? Blown-in insulation?"

"That's the least of it." Tim brushed at the tiny white balls on his jacket. "We were just setting up to take out the old ductwork over on Harris Street, and half the ceiling came down on us."

"Is anyone hurt?"

"Nah, it just crumbled away. Apparently, there's been bats living in there for a long time."

"Oh." She couldn't help it. She took a step backward. "You're all covered with bat... er, guano."

"Yeah, bat guano." One of the men snorted and then coughed.

"Histoplasmosis."

Eleanor turned to the speaker. He held up his phone. "I googled it. It's a lung disease you get from inhaling bat... guano."

She groaned. "Okay, you'd better all go over to Occupational Health and get checked out. Let me grab the paperwork. Umm... how about if you guys wait out here. I'll be right back."

Tim gave a bark of laughter. "Hurry. By the way, you have company."

Eleanor stopped at the sight of her visitor, a fatalistic sort of acceptance rendering her speechless.

"She's says she's your sister-in-law."

"I can get you a job." Laurie stood in the middle of the room while Eleanor printed out copies of accident reports and claims forms. "A real job."

"I have a job, Laurie, and I need to do it right now. All those men are waiting for me. Then I need to call Uncle Gary and see if I need to call our lawyer."

"But, Eleanor, this isn't what you went to school for. I know you wanted a break, but this..." Laurie swept out her arms, encompassing the noisome men outside as well as the utilitarian office. "Wouldn't you rather have a job in my office or as a substitute somewhere until you decide what you want to do?"

"No." She couldn't do this right now. Of all the rotten timing... Eleanor straightened and stared at her sister-in-law. "I am not going to your workshop tomorrow, Laurie."

The other woman stiffened. "It's such a good opportunity for you, Eleanor. You'd make valuable connections. Tomorrow's Saturday, so you won't miss any work here."

"I'm busy all day tomorrow." Eleanor couldn't help smiling at the words. She set the stapler on the desk. "Can you take a paper from each stack, in that order, and staple them together, please?"

Laurie complied, continuing her appeal as she worked. "You know, you could probably get a job up here, if you just want to get out of the cities."

"I have a job up here." Eleanor tried to soften her voice. The compromise was an improvement over the usual insistence that she live near the rest of them. "I like my job, Laurie. I really do. I know you don't understand that, but it's true. It's not always like this. Most of the time, it's very interesting work, building things. When it's not so busy, maybe I can show you what we do."

"No! I don't want to see what you do!" Laurie stomped her foot like a child. "I want you to come to your senses and come home where you belong! And can you please take off that stupid hat?"

17

Make sure you get some of my mom's chicken hotdish," Sarah said. "Everyone loves it. She always makes three pans full, and there's never any leftovers."

"Thanks for the tip." Eleanor smiled at her young cousin. "Anything else I should know?"

The little girl beckoned her downward and whispered. "Mrs. Jessin makes cookies with whole wheat flour and doesn't add sugar to them."

"Good to know. Thank you."

"They're pretty bad," Sarah said seriously. "They're nutritious, though."

"Well, I'm not eating them." Eleanor shuddered dramatically. "What kind of cookies are made with whole wheat flour and no sugar?"

"We call that whole wheat bread," Jeffrey said, "but it's worse because it's masquerading as a cookie."

Eleanor turned to smile up at him and nearly dropped her plate. "What happened to you?"

"Sarah beat me up."

His sister heaved an exasperated sigh. "Will you stop telling people that? It's embarrassing."

Jeffrey shook his head. "Not for me. It's a lot less embarrassing to be beat up by your eight-year-old sister than to tell people what really happened." He touched the strip of tape over his nose. "With that gash in my forehead, I might have a scar like Harry Potter. At least only one of my eyes is swollen. I can still see out of the other one."

"It's very colorful," Eleanor said. "What did really happen? Will you tell me, if I promise to keep it a secret?"

"Yeah, it's not really a secret. I just like to tease Sarah." He looked over the fellowship hall and pointed. "There's Penny over there. Come on, Sarah. You know mom won't let you eat all three of those brownies. You'd better give me one."

She loved this place. The whole church treated her as if she belonged there. She'd never lived there, but they treated her as if she'd come home. Maybe she had.

"Hi, Eleanor!" Penny stood to give her a hug. "We live in the same house, and I never see you. We'll have to make an appointment to get together soon."

"Yes, let's do that, this week," Eleanor said. She sat next to Sarah and looked at Jeffrey. "Okay, I'm ready."

"It's really Penny's fault. She wanted Mom to go to some bridal thing in the cities, and then Adrienne and Sarah wanted to go, too, so I had to milk the goat and take care of the chickens. And you know how that goes. That little Rhode Island Red took off." Jeffrey shook his head in disgust. "How can something with six-inch-long legs outrun a human being? I almost had her, in the yard, because the snow slowed her down, but she made it to the driveway and went crazy, running back and forth. I started thinking of 'why did the chicken cross the road' jokes and was laughing so hard I didn't see Rocky coming."

"That's the red rooster," Sarah informed Eleanor. "He's mean."

"I grabbed that big coaster sled and was using it like

a shield, to keep him back," Jeffrey continued.

"What were you using for a sword?" Penny asked.

Jeffrey grinned. "A snowshoe. I didn't want to hurt him—much. Anyhow, he kept coming on, and I was backing up—"

"Getting closer to the hill?" Penny asked innocently. She was already giggling. "You slid down the hill, didn't you?"

"Don't ruin my story. It's marginally less humiliating if I made a dramatic telling of it." Jeffrey made a face at his sister. "So, I was busy fighting the rooster, and out of the corner of my eye, I see the hen coming at me from the other side, right under my feet. I kind of twisted around, trying to avoid her and Rocky, and I fell on the sled, sort of sideways." He wiggled in his chair to demonstrate. "I swear... Rocky pushed me down the hill. I didn't get far before I rolled over and whapped myself in the face with the edge of the snowshoe." He held the side of his hand to his face. "A straight line down the middle of my face."

"You hit yourself in the face with a snowshoe?" Sarah sounded disgusted. Then she laughed. Eleanor couldn't help laughing with her.

Jeffrey looked resigned. "Well, it's all true."

Eleanor reached across the table and patted his hand. "Corroborative detail, intended to give artistic verisimilitude to an otherwise bald and unconvincing narrative."

They all stared at her.

"Say that again?" Jeffrey asked.

She repeated it. "It's from 'The Mikado.' Gilbert and Sullivan."

"Corroborative detail, to give artistic verisimilitude

to an otherwise bald..." Jeffrey broke off.

Eleanor said it again, and he practiced it until he could quote it smoothly. She laughed at his pleasure in the quotation. "You homeschoolers do know how to have a good time."

"It's a great quote," Jeffrey said. "I'm going to use it. You're a good teacher, Eleanor."

"I found you a coach," Larry said. "A police officer who played basketball in high school and college. He's committed to every Sunday afternoon through the end of the school year. So, you'll be able to be more of an assistant and work with the boys."

David slid into the booth. "That's great! When can he start?"

"He's going to come and just hang out today, but if everybody's happy, he can start officially next weekend." He lifted his coffee cup in salute. "I'm paying him."

"Paying him? It's supposed to be a ministry!"

Larry propped his elbow on the table and rested his chin on his hand. "David, this is your ministry, but it got too big, and now you don't have a ministry. You have a nice secular program. You just organize and supervise."

"But you can't go on paying him indefinitely, and I don't know how much I can contribute, if I -" David broke off. If he became a pastor. Not when. A check in the spirit or spiritual warfare? The more he thought and prayed and read, the more conflicted he became.

Larry waited patiently, drinking his coffee and looking out the window.

"Do you think I'm wrong? About being a pastor?" David hadn't meant to ask him, but what was the point of having a Christian psychologist for a best friend if you couldn't get free advice? He tried to think of something funny to say about that, but he couldn't. "I just don't know anymore."

"Have you tried making a list with pros and cons?"

David paused. "That's your best psychiatric advice and spiritual counsel? Make a list?"

"I'll try to come up with something profound if the list fails." Larry set down his cup. "I see you wanting to serve God in an active kind of capacity. You like the one-on-one of working with the boys at basketball. You get pretty pumped up about the Jesus People kind of ministry." He held up a hand. "I am not telling you to run away and become a hippie. Please don't. And I'm not saying you shouldn't become a pastor. I'm just saying—because I know you're already praying about it—make a list or two, with pros and cons, about what you would do as a pastor, or in some other kind of ministry, or even doing what you do now with worship music and activities for the kids. Look at it analytically. You're an engineer." He grinned. "That'll be five cents, please."

Cal leaned over David's chair and peered at the computer screen. "How's that going? Did you find a way to make it lighter?"

"Maybe. I tried this." David clicked to a different window. "And it works, but I don't like the aesthetics. It's not quite right. But we can use it if I don't come up with something else."

"Take your time. We're not out for the quick buck." Cal put a hand on his shoulder. "You do good work, and even though you don't like them, you're my best guy for presentations. I think you got Frans Brown hooked."

"Excellent!" David grinned. "It's not so much doing the presentation as wearing the suit and tie. Why do we have to do that?"

"No idea, but it is what it is. I like it better when you wear the suit. You're better with people, anyhow. So, I fully expect to be signing a contract next week, and I'd like you to come along." He scowled. "Angela quit."

"Quit! I didn't know that." David leaned back in his chair, watching his boss. Cal looked like a sulking baby. I don't know what I'm supposed to do now. She says she'll come back this summer for a while, to train someone new, but I don't know how to find someone to replace her. I don't even know what she does."

"Maybe you could get her to write up a job description and help with the hiring," David suggested. "Or ask Andrea." Andrea was the office manager, wasn't she? Or maybe she was the administrative assistant.

Cal pulled over a chair and sat down. "Andrea does different stuff. You know what Angela was?"

David shook his head. "No," he said truthfully. He hadn't even realized she was an employee until Larry told him.

"Angela was the CEO."

Wow. That was a shocker. "I thought you were the CEO."

Cal lifted his glasses and rubbed the bridge of his nose. "I am. I mean, that's my title, but you know I'm not CEO material. I just want to be an engineer. I nearly ran us into the ground. When Angela graduated from college, Mom insisted I give her a job. I didn't think I'd have anything for her to do. I didn't even know if I could keep the business afloat." He gave a reminiscent grin. "A month after she got here, she had all the books in order. Six months after that, she was running the place and we were making a profit. She's a genius.'

"But she quit." David hoped that didn't mean his job was in jeopardy. "What's she doing now?"

"Larry took her away, and he won't tell me or Meg where she is." He leaned back and crossed his arms over his chest. "I think she's in some kind of a sanitarium or something. Like I said, she'll come back here in the summer, but then she's going back to college. She wants to be a doctor. Not an ordinary doctor, like you go to when you're sick. She wants to do something with 'bacterial research'." He said the last two words in a sneer. "She already had a useful degree."

David looked at Cal. A genius with no people skills and little concern for the health of his sister. He'd skimmed right over the sanitarium and on to his own grievance. David hoped Angela found work that would fulfill her — and work for which she'd be recognized.

"If we weren't all Christians," Penny said, "I'd say Aunt Violet's part witch. She's got this uncanny ability to read people and tell the future. You know those quilts she makes?"

Eleanor nodded. "Yes, they're all over the house."

"She made a block for me, of course. You know

what was on it? Clothes from Brian's childhood. All those years ago, she'd decided that I'd eventually marry him."

"You're kidding!" Eleanor sat up straight.

"I'd show you, but she still has it." Penny laughed. "She's probably adding my children as we speak. I wonder if I'm having boys or girls."

"Hmm... I wonder if she's started mine yet. I'd like to know the future." Would she? Yes, Eleanor decided. She would.

"I've been wondering... do you think she's doing okay? Mentally, I mean?" Penny twisted the cap of her water bottle. "It might be my imagination, but she seems quieter lately."

"I don't know what she was like before I came here," Eleanor said. "She's really sharp with things that matter to her—the genealogy, quilting, and things like that. She knows what she wants to do for a garden this year."

"Maybe she's hoping to dig up more family treasure. Last year, she found—or rather, Brian found—an old Swedish bridal crown that her father made for her mother before they were married." Penny smiled. "And a love letter to go with it. Brian read it to me when he proposed."

"I saw a picture of it," Eleanor said, "and a copy of the letter. It's so romantic, and sad, too, knowing that she died in childbirth."

"They did have some time together. They were friends for ten years before they got married, and they were married for nearly twenty years. That's pretty good by today's standards."

"True." Eleanor snuggled back into the corner of the couch, tucking her stockinged feet underneath her. "Why do you think Aunt Violet never married? Kristina never did, either, but she sounds awful."

"I don't know," Penny said. "Violet worked for the phone company, you know, as an operator. Maybe she just never met the right man."

"Their lives don't seem to have been very happy. Linnea escaped at the first opportunity. I think if I'd been Violet, I wouldn't have been too fussy about finding Mr. Right."

"Aunt Violet? Are you in here?"

"Hello, dear."

Eleanor turned on the light, and her aunt blinked. "Sorry, I didn't mean to blind you. She turned on a table lamp and flicked off the light switch. "I forget how bright that one is."

"Brian put daylight LED bulbs in everything. Penny and I have been quietly replacing them with soft whites, but I keep forgetting to do that one."

"Are you okay, sitting here in the dark?" Eleanor dropped onto one of the old-fashioned wing chairs.

"Praying. Thinking about the past, praying about the future. Trying to give it all to God to worry about instead of taking it on myself." Violet smiled. "And praying for you. We really haven't talked about God much, have we? You come to church and sound like a believer, but I don't know much about your faith."

"Yes, I'm a believer." Eleanor said the word again. "Believer." It sounded like belonging. She believed in Jesus, belonged to Him.

"So, did you grow up in a Christian home?"

"We went to church most weekends, when I was little, but we got busy with sports and things later," Eleanor explained. She hated making her parents sound bad—and Aunt Violet would think poorly of her parents for skipping church in favor of sports—but she needed to be honest. "And I went to youth group for a while in junior high. I did confirmation."

"But were you saved?" Violet pressed. "I don't know the terminology people use today. Were you born again? Converted?"

Eleanor furrowed her brow. "Well, yes, but... you mean, was there one time that I did all of that at once and understood it? I sort of knew it, growing up, and then we went over it all again in confirmation classes. We had to say if we believed it or not, and then we could join the church."

"Did you—do you believe it?"

"Yes, I do. I think I understand what you're talking about. There was a little girl in one of my classes who told me she invited Jesus into her heart. I asked a friend about it, because I was afraid it might be something weird." That memory reminded her of meeting David at the coffee shop.

"Yes. Did you have a time like that?" Violet asked.

Eleanor shook her head slowly. "I don't think I had any one magical epiphany moment. Was I supposed to? It just kind of clarified over time, over the last few months. I knew all the basic facts, and it's like things just clicked into place a bit at a time. I started understanding sin more—if you know what I mean. Not like the little girl who was seeing sin as being naughty or telling a lie. So, then I could see the holiness of God. Salvation wasn't a light thing—not a quick, cheap forgiveness."

"The gift of grace is very precious," said Violet. "His

blood, poured out for us."

"Right. And then when we were at church, and later, when I did some reading on my own, I just kept seeing the bigger picture. And I realized I'll never see the whole picture until I'm in Heaven." She smiled at her aunt. "Until I go Home."

"Glory, glory." Violet's words were just a whisper.

Eleanor continued. "I knew the words since I was little—saved by grace through faith, the grace of God that brings salvation, if we confess our sins, he forgives—even though I hadn't thought about them in a long time." She tapped her chest. "They were still 'in there.'" She tipped her head to one side, considering. "It's almost like they were big words. I knew what they meant all along, but as I got older—mostly in the last few months—my vocabulary and comprehension skills increased, and they started to make more sense."

"And the better you understand God's word, the more you know Him and love Him. You can't have a close relationship with someone you don't know."

"Very true." Eleanor stood up. "So that's where I stand, Aunt Violet. I'm reading and praying and listening at church. The Holy Spirit keeps pretty busy, convicting me of something new every time I turn around, but it's all good. God's good." She dropped to her knees by the old woman's chair and hugged her.

"Glory, glory." Aunt Violet's words made Eleanor think of the quilts. She'd ask her about that later.

18

David knew how to pray. He did it all the time. He was doing it now. Larry was right... why did he need a class in prayer? David worked his way through the test. The definitions were all so similar, each with just a small difference in nuance. But those differences mattered.

He wondered what Eleanor was doing. She'd been... adorable at the job site last Friday. She'd been trying to be professional, of course, and she really was. But with the hard hat sliding all over her head, she did look a bit like a bobble head doll. A beautiful bobble head doll.

Outside the testing room, the reference librarian stamped books with vigor, branding them for return if they tried to escape. A little girl skipped back and forth between the rows of books. When she stopped and made a face at him through the window, he made one back. She ran away.

He had to focus. This final exam, unlike most of the tests for his online classes, required paper and pencil, a proctor and a ticking clock. He bent over the test, completing and reviewing the answers until the librarian tapped on the door. "You have five minutes left."

"I'm done." David stood up and handed her the sheaf of papers. "Thank you."

"You're welcome." She led the way to the reference

desk. "I'll just sign off on this and seal up the envelope for you. You have the postage ready? There you go! It will go out with the morning mail." She beamed at him. "Mostly, we get homeschoolers in here. College students usually use the university library."

"My classes are online, through a school in Virginia," David said. "And I'm almost done."

"Well, I hope this goes well for you." She held up the envelope.

"Thanks." He cracked open one of the glass doors to inhale fresh air. The black sky and bright stars promised a cold night outside the overheated library. Slipping on his coat, he turned back to nod goodbye to the librarian. She stood outside the other testing room in conversation with a young blond woman. Eleanor.

He pulled on one of his gloves. He should leave before she saw him, avoiding embarrassment for both of them. He should do it quickly. Just walk out the door.

He stepped toward Eleanor.

"David." She held out her hand, not surprised to see him. She'd probably seen him through the glass of the testing room earlier. "Nice to see you. Do you come here often?" She laughed at the cliché pickup line. "Let me rephrase that. Do you use this library frequently?"

"No, hardly ever. What are you doing out here?" It felt good to talk with her again. "What's a nice girl like you doing in a place like this?"

She tipped her head toward the testing room. "My cousin Jeffrey has a test. He does some online courses, and he didn't get to the Milaca library before they closed. We raced out here." She glanced at her phone. "He's barely got enough time to finish it here."

"Ah. One of the homeschoolers the librarian

mentioned. He takes college classes online while he's finishing high school?"

She nodded. "It's a smart plan. I wish I'd done that."

"I'm surprised you didn't, coming from a family of educators."

"I took a lot of AP and Honors classes instead, another year of Spanish and some music electives. All very useful."

He raised his brows. "Do I hear sarcasm? What would you have liked to take, other than early college credits?"

"Auto repair, for one thing. My car is making a squealing noise. Uncle Gary said I can use his, but I'd rather not. I need to ask Uncle Carl or Jeffrey." She scowled. It was a cute scowl. "Everyone should take a class in auto repair."

"I agree. Would you like me to take a look at it?" He hadn't meant to say that, but it was too late to take it back. "I'm a mechanical engineer. Mechanical, mechanic, auto mechanic? Engineer, engine? I'm not making any promises, but I could take a look."

Her eyes had a faint wash of green over the blue tonight, probably from the fluorescent lights. "No. I can't ask that of you. David, I am so, so sorry. I was wrong, and you were all right. I wish... I wish I hadn't done that."

"Please let me." David moderated his eager tone and responded to the apology. "No hard feelings. I can at least take a look, to see if it's safe to drive. Is it in the parking lot now?"

She shook her head. "No, we took Jeffrey's. He can drive at night with a licensed adult driver. I feel old."

It was just as well. In the cold, dark night, with only the few tools he kept in the truck, he wouldn't be able to see or do much.

"I could take it to work tomorrow, but I won't get there until nearly one o'clock." She smiled. A warm smile, not the dazzling one or the mischievous one. "On Tuesday mornings, I play the piano for the Golden Oldies sing-along at the nursing home where Uncle Gary and my Uncle Olof are."

"I bet that's fun!"

"It really is. I only agreed to do it because Uncle Gary's shoulder was broken, but I love it. He still leads the singing."

Maybe he should go visit his good friend, Gary, in the nursing home tomorrow. "I didn't realize he was still there."

"I think they have to chain him to the bed at night, so he doesn't escape. He's ready to leave, as soon as they release him."

"I'll come out at one o'clock tomorrow and take a look at it." David sat down, compelling her to do the same, not above taking advantage of her good manners. "Look, Eleanor. There's no reason we can't be friends. Not every relationship has to end in traditional marriage. Not all relationships should." He wished this one had been going that direction, though.

"I was at fault, David. It was selfish of me. I'm sorry." She pushed a strand of hair back from her face. "I'm upset with myself and embarrassed about the whole thing."

"Well, it's over. We can have a good laugh about it someday. Maybe not this week, or this month…"

"Or this year," Eleanor interrupted. "Thank you. I appreciate your willingness to let bygones be bygones. I didn't mean to -"

It was his turn to interrupt. "Let's just drop it. Let's pretend we met at the coffeehouse that day Larry broke your mouse."

A genuine smile lit her face. "Okay. I got a much nicer mouse with the money he gave me."

"Good. You should have kept all of it. Larry can afford it. He makes about three times what I do, and he's always looking for opportunities to do good."

"I'll keep that in mind," she said.

She was smiling. He should leave while the going was good. "I'll be there at one tomorrow."

"I'll pack a lunch for both of us. Do you like peanut butter?"

"Of course, I like peanut butter. I was a poor starving college student for five years. I did get enough of ramen noodles, though, so don't bring those."

"I ate in the cafeteria," Eleanor said, "so I didn't have those. I was going to stock up on them in case I stayed at the cabin, but now that I live with Aunt Violet, I've been eating pretty well. I just like peanut butter sandwiches, so that's what I normally bring for lunch."

"Works for me. See you then."

Eleanor watched David leave the library, hastily, as if afraid she'd change her mind. He'd been gracious about the matchmaking business. Had he told the people at Betwixt Two Hearts about her deception and requested another match? She hoped he'd find one. He would make a good husband.

"Who was that?"

"A friend." Eleanor waited while the librarian sealed up Jeffrey's test. "How do you think you did?"

"Oh, fine. Piece of cake." Jeffrey zipped up his hoodie. "I didn't know you had any friends."

"Thanks a lot!"

"I didn't mean that. I just didn't think you knew many people here. You work for Uncle Gary in the office and you live with Aunt Violet."

"That does sound pretty pathetic, doesn't it?"

Jeffrey cast an anxious glance at her. "Sorry. I didn't mean it like that."

"Well, don't keep explaining. It gets worse every time. Are you driving?"

"Absolutely."

She followed him outside, marveling at his bare legs. Did boys around here wear cargo shorts as some kind of macho symbol? "Aren't you cold?"

"The car warms up pretty fast."

"I mean, your shorts. Aren't your legs cold?"

He glanced down as if surprised by his attire. "Oh, no. I'm good. I thought you meant you were cold. The car gets warm fast. It's not one of those new ones with heated seats, though."

"Just wondered. I've seen a lot of teenage boys with shorts on, all winter."

"Yeah, we're tough." Jeffrey smirked. "We only wear jeans when we're doing stuff outside, not just going in and out of buildings."

The boy drove competently, as he did most things. She wished she could ask him about his education. Her parents made a point of not discussing the homeschooling Andersons, tight-lipped and tactful. They probably saw it as a rejection of the very things they devoted their lives to.

That was probably how they saw her behavior, too. A rejection.

"So, are you ever going to be a teacher again?"

The question startled her. She glanced at his profile. He looked relaxed, with hands at ten o'clock and two o'clock, his slender neck revealing his youth even in silhouette, in the dark.

"Maybe. I don't know yet."

"Did you like it?"

"No." Her answer startled her as much as his question had. It was easier, in the dark car, on a quiet road, to be honest. And Jeffrey wouldn't pressure her to be something he wanted her to be. He didn't care what she did. It was a refreshing change. "No, I didn't like it."

"But you thought you would?" He asked. "That's what you went to school for? You got all the way through college and then found out you didn't like it?"

"Sort of." She tried to find helpful words. These were important matters for a boy his age. "By the time I graduated, I was beginning to think I'd made a mistake. Then I taught school for a few years, and I was sure of it."

"All my siblings are in the medical field. Lisa's nearly done with her nursing degree. Jeremy's a respiratory therapist, and Mark's on his way to med school. He wants to be some kind of surgeon."

And it made her mother crazy that they were all so academically successful. Eleanor smiled in the dark.

"Adrienne doesn't know whether she wants to be a medical missionary or an actress," Jeffrey went on, "but I'm just not interested in blood and guts. I thought I might want to be a lawyer, probably because it goes with doctors. I told Mark I'd defend him when he cut off the wrong body parts and got sued for malpractice."

"You could give him a family discount," Eleanor said lightly. "Handy to have a lawyer in the family."

"According to my mom, it would be more handy to have a plumber. She's thrilled that Penny's marrying Brian, because he's an electrician. Well, an electrical engineer, but he has practical skills, too."

Eleanor laughed. It was the funniest thing she'd heard in ages. Brian had gone to college for five years, to earn an advanced degree in engineering, and his future mother-in-law was glad he had some practical skills. "The degree isn't worth much if it doesn't come with some useful skills, is it?"

Jeffrey ignored her hilarity. "I liked speech and debate, and I didn't want to be a politician or economist, so I thought maybe law..."

"Jeffrey, are you really interested in law?"

"I don't think so." He stopped to wait for another car and glanced at her. "I think I'd really like to do landscaping. Maybe do some more nursery stuff, too."

"I think that sounds like interesting work." He wanted to follow in his father's footsteps; she didn't want to follow in hers. "You've done a lot of it, right? So, you probably have an idea of what's involved."

"All my life. Dad says he'll take me on as a junior partner if I still want it after I go to college."

"Would you take business classes? Horticulture?"

"Yeah." He drove in silence for a while and then said, "Dad didn't make Penny finish college, but that was different. I think I'll go for all four years."

"A business degree would be helpful," Eleanor said. She wasn't qualified to give educational advice. Or was she? She turned in her seat to face him more fully. "Business and horticulture would both be useful, but talk to people who are actually successful in those fields—not just a college counselor. Get advice on what works best for you in your own situation, with a family business. You don't want a cookie-cutter education. Everyone's needs are different."

"Uh, Eleanor, we're homeschooled. Not a lot of cookie-cutting going on in the Anderson household. But thanks. My brothers and Lisa have all complained about the classes they had to take—and the ones that looked interesting but they weren't allowed to take, or didn't fit into their schedules."

"One of my friends took a class in internet security," Eleanor said. "I asked my counselor about it, and he said I couldn't take it. I wasn't in the program, or I didn't have room for an elective, or something like that. Someday, when my email gets hacked, I'm going to go back and find that guy."

"Everyone should know internet security," Jeffrey said seriously, "but there's thousands of people at colleges. I suppose they do the best they can, trying to get everyone the classes they need for their degrees. My friends in the public schools say the same thing. They get on a certain track and then can't do anything else."

The best they can. She almost wished her parents were able to hear this boy's comments. He should get on a committee for education reform.

"It must drive Aunt Kathy crazy that she can't solve all those problems. She really cares about kids and education."

Eleanor felt a tiny—very tiny—twinge of guilt. Her mother did care. She was single-minded because she cared about kids and education. She devoted all her time and attention to her work because she cared about kids and education. She thought Eleanor should be a teacher because she cared about kids and education more than she cared about what Eleanor wanted. Eleanor would rather plant trees with Jeffrey. Or learn how to plan and build structures with Uncle Gary.

"So, what do you want to do if you don't want to be a teacher?" her cousin asked.

"Well, I've been thinking about that a lot."

"What do you like to do for fun?"

"Fun? I'm not sure." That was a good question. Eleanor thought about it. "I like music and concerts and art museums."

"Really?" He sounded skeptical.

"Really! I wish I got outside more."

"Why don't you?" asked Jeffrey. "You can always just go out for a walk."

"It's cold out!"

"It's Minnesota!"

The absurdity of her objection struck her. Unless she moved south, she should find something to do outdoors even when the weather wasn't warm. "What do you do in the winter?"

"Skiing and snowmobiling and fishing. We go sledding sometimes, sometimes with chickens." He made clucking noises and continued. "We've got snowshoes, as you know, but we haven't used them much. There's a skating rink in town, in the park, but you can just get outside at home. When my brothers were around more, we used to make labyrinths of tunnels in the snow. Last week, my friend and I made forts in the backyard, for a snowball fight, and then Sadie wanted to turn one of them into an igloo." He chuckled. "Mom turned it into a science experiment and social studies lesson, of course, but it was still fun. She made the igloo, and then her friend came over and wanted her own house. So, they made her a little house and then they wanted a bigger one. So, they're building an entire neighborhood in the backyard, with paths for roads and little snowmen people."

Fascinated, Eleanor asked, "and they just play out there?"

Her own childhood had been enriched by team sports, music, clubs, and other scheduled fun. If her brothers had ever played like the Anderson kids, she hadn't seen it. Of course, they lived in town, and they were all so busy. Her mom said it was good to keep kids busy, to keep them out of trouble.

"I guess I could take up snowman construction," she said.

"Hey! You could make a giant bride in the front yard of the farmhouse, with a fancy wedding dress. I bet we could give it a lot of detail. You can use water to help shape the snow. That would be awesome!"

Jeffrey's enthusiasm was tempting, but Eleanor shook her head. "Your sister's worked awfully hard to overcome the farm image for her bridal salon. She likes the snow in the front yard to be smooth. We stay on the sidewalks. But we could do it in the backyard!"

"Not nearly as much fun," Jeffrey said. "So, do you think you'll keep working for Uncle Gary, then?" He took a turn a little too fast and cast a guilty glance in her direction. "Sorry."

"I think so. I like it," she said, "and I think I'm good at it."

19

Eleanor turned her back to the wind, holding her hair out of her face with mittened hands. A hat would have been sensible, but they always made a mess of her hair. David leaned over the engine, apparently oblivious to the January cold.

"Can you tell what's wrong with it?" Her teeth were chattering, bringing memories of the first time she met him here.

"I think so. Go start it up."

Eleanor opened the car door and slid inside. "Okay, step back." She waited for him to move.

"Start it up," he shouted.

She leaned out the door. "I'm waiting for you to move. I don't want you to get hurt when I start it."

He walked around to where she was. "Okay, I'm here. Now start the engine."

Was he laughing at her? Eleanor complied and sat in the car while David examined the running engine, unable to watch him poking around the moving parts. Odd... She'd been willing to let Uncle Carl do it.

She turned off the engine and slid from the car. "Is it terminal?"

"Only in the battery." David closed the hood.

"The battery?"

He grinned. "Terminals, battery, get it?"

Eleanor shook her head.

"You can't tell me you don't know how to use jumper cables," David said.

"Oh! Battery terminals. Yes, I've done that! My roommate and I had to jumpstart her car when she left the lights on. We found a YouTube video."

"A YouTube video. Well, that was resourceful."

"That's the real thing we need to teach people," she informed him loftily. "How to find the information they need to know. Always start with Google."

"It's a good place to start." He tossed his tool bag in the back of his truck. "Where can I wash up?"

"Inside. We can eat at the conference table." She chuckled. "That's what Uncle Gary calls it, but it's really just one of those collapsible white plastic tables. We keep it in the closet and bring it out for special occasions."

"Like lunch with your favorite mechanic." David gave a little bow and held up his greasy hands. "Where's the washroom?"

"So, is it going to be expensive?" Eleanor opened a container of grapes and set it between them. "Please tell me it won't be expensive."

"I don't think it will be expensive. It looks like your fan belt's loose. I can put a new one on for you. If that doesn't fix it, it might be one of the other belts.

So, it's something that can be changed at home?"

"If it's a belt." He took a sandwich and peeked under the top slice of bread. "Crunchy or creamy?"

"Crunchy, of course," Eleanor said.

"Of course. It's awfully nice of you to make lunch for me," David said.

"It's more nice of you to look at my car. I really appreciate it. I'm always asking Uncle Gary to do favors for me. He says he doesn't mind, but... I don't like being indebted to people."

"Well, this makes us even." David held up the sandwich. "Thank you."

"You're a cheap date." Eleanor bit into her sandwich, wishing she'd not said that.

"I like peanut butter sandwiches. They remind me of youth and college."

She rolled her eyes. "You aren't exactly middle-aged." Ugh. They had to get off the topics related to the matchmaking agency. "Aunt Violet and I are still learning how to handle meals. She's never lived on her own before. She grew up in the farmhouse and lived there with the entire family—about 15 people—until she retired, then she moved into a house in town with her brother, and then she moved in with my Grandma, and when Grandma moved to Florida, Aunt Violet moved in with Uncle Carl. Now she's nearly 90, and she's living alone, back in the farmhouse. In the annex, anyhow. Penny lives upstairs in the farmhouse, but they both have separate entrances."

"But you're living with her," David pointed out, "so she's still not really living alone."

"She says she is, because it's her house. She invited me as a guest. A temporary guest." She laughed at the expression on his face. "Yes, that's what she said: a temporary guest. I wonder what she'll really think of living alone, when she does it.

"She never married and had kids of her own?"

"No, never." Eleanor folded up her paper napkin. "But she's always had nieces and nephews—and grand-nieces and grand-nephews—living with her, and she was like another grandma to them. I never knew her very well, of course. I'd only met her a few times."

"And here you are, living with her."

"She seems to think it's normal," Eleanor said, "and my options are pretty limited right now. I needed something in a hurry, when Uncle Gary went in the hospital, and she took me in. I need to find a place of my own soon."

"Does that mean you're staying here?

"Yes," Eleanor said. "I am. I'm going to take a permanent job with Uncle Gary. I like it here."

He smiled, creases forming at the corners of his brown-green eyes. "I'm glad."

When she said it was the original family farmhouse, he'd assumed it looked like most midwestern farmhouses: two-story frame houses with shabby white paint and a peeling porch with overgrown shrubbery and a rutted driveway leading around back to a pole barn twice the size of the house.

This was bigger and looked more like a business than a home, with a Penny Anderson Designs sign suspended from a wrought iron frame. A bridal shop.

David stepped from his truck onto smooth blacktop. Two other cars sat at the end of the little parking lot. Brides? He grimaced, glad he wouldn't have to go inside. Eleanor said it was an annex, with a separate entrance.

The back yard was friendlier, with a patio and fire pit. Trees and piles of frozen leaves edged the lawn, still bare and muddy in February.

"Can I help you?"

David turned to see a blond woman in a blue and white plaid coat. "I'm looking for Eleanor Nielson. Is she here?"

"No, she's out of town. Can I help you with something?" Her expression conveyed annoyance rather than any desire to be helpful.

"Are you Penny?"

The girl shook her head. "Brittany Green. I'm a friend of Eleanor's."

"She's mentioned you." David took a step forward, hand outstretched. "I'm David Reid."

"Oh." She walked forward slowly and shook his hand. "Eleanor's gone to Minneapolis for her parents' anniversary."

"Already? I'd hoped to catch her before she left."

"Were you going to go?" Brittany tipped her head and regarded him with interest. "She said you weren't."

He shook his head. "I ran into her uncle at a job site, and he said she was going alone. He's worried about her car and asked me to drop off a charging kit."

"Drop it off? Don't you live in St. Cloud?"

He rubbed his jaw. "Gary's busy, after being out of work for so long. I had some spare time." He'd offered to do it, pretending to believe that Gary's thinly-disguised attempt at matchmaking was a genuine request for a favor.

He wasn't as sure of his own motives or feelings. Now he'd wished he'd come yesterday, just in case she really did have car trouble.

"You missed her."

He did miss her. Even with their brief acquaintance, with few conversations and the issues between them, he missed her. "Can I leave the charging kit here? It's in my truck."

"Sure." Brittany gestured for him to precede her. "You never know... she might really have a need for it." Her tone indicated skepticism.

"I've never been here before," he said over his shoulder. "It's not what I expected from an old family farmhouse."

"It's mostly the bridal salon, and Penny's family can do anything. Gary has the construction business, and Penny's dad is a landscaper. Her fiancé is an electrical engineer and all-around handyman," Brittany said. "The inside is beautiful. Would you like to see it?"

Not really. He shook his head. "I'd probably better get back to work."

"Oh, come on. You drove all the way out here. You might as well come inside for a few minutes." She grabbed his elbow and tugged. "There aren't any brides in there — just Penny and Violet. We were eating lunch and saw you come in the yard. Violet wanted to point a shotgun at you for trespassing."

Brittany, Penny and Violet. He'd rather face the shotgun. "I don't think so."

"They don't know about the online dating. They think you and Eleanor know each other through Gary and her work there." She smiled. "You're just friends."

Well, that was what Eleanor had wanted: friends.

No, she'd wanted a date for a party, as if Betwixt Two Hearts was an escort service. He'd been mad, hurt, humiliated, and disappointed. And the next time he saw her, in that ridiculous hard hat, all of those things melted away.

She tugged again. "Come on. Look—there's Violet, peeking out from behind that lace curtain." She waved at the old woman, who beckoned in response.

He gave up. "Okay, but just for a few minutes. I don't think Eleanor would like it." The word 'stalker' occurred to him, but he was on a semi-legitimate errand for her uncle, after all, and he'd met Violet in the hospital. It would be rude to ignore her.

That hadn't taken long. The old lady's interrogation techniques should earn her a place in the FBI. The younger women sipped their coffee politely and murmured encouragement as he told Violet about his family, his faith, his goals, and everything else she wanted to know. So far, she hadn't asked about Eleanor.

He shot a harried glance at Brittany, who smiled blandly and tucked a stray strand of hair behind her ear. "You know, you're lucky to have such a supportive family. I'm feeling bad for Eleanor right now." Her limpid blue eyes met his. "Those people will eat her alive."

"Nonsense!" Violet set her cup on the table, missing the saucer. "They're a fine family. You've never even met them."

"I know what Eleanor tells me," Brittany retorted.

David admired her courage and hoped she survived

the discussion. Her desire to throw barbs at him—totally unjustified—had led Brittany to disparage Violet's family. He resisted the urge to smirk at her.

Brittany continued. "She keeps saying, 'I know they love me', 'I know they want what's best for me', 'they're really nice people', and so on, over and over, but they don't understand her or respect her."

Violet frowned. "What do you mean, they don't respect her? Of course, they respect her. They love her."

"They call her all the time," Brittany said, "and they send her emails with job openings—teaching jobs, in the cities. She's told them she doesn't want to be a teacher, and they treat her like an obstinate child, humoring her for a little while and then dragging her back into good behavior."

"They are kind of pushy," Penny said. "Aunt Kathy used to quiz us, as if she thought we might be behind in school. Adrienne and I ran away and hid whenever she was here. Lisa always got stuck with her, because she was too nice to avoid it."

"Kathy was a nice girl," Violet said. "She was."

"Mom finally told her to leave us alone. She said we weren't trained seals." Penny chuckled. "Later, Aunt Kathy sent her a list of private schools in the area, 'just in case.'"

"And this," Brittany put in, "is where Eleanor would say 'I know they just want the best for me.'"

They seemed to have forgotten him. He took a drink of his coffee and kept quiet.

"I know she was upset with Laurie about this party," Penny said. "She said she was praying for a blizzard."

"So, she wouldn't have to go. Laurie's the worst of

the bunch. She's one of those super-achiever, perfect people who make everyone else look bad." Brittany snorted. "She insisted on having this big party with expensive gifts for a 35th wedding anniversary, and she called Eleanor every other day, telling her all the details."

"That girl has a whole nest of issues," Aunt Violet said. "She's the most insecure person I've ever met."

"Insecure?" Penny asked. "I've only met her once. She seemed more than confident. She's got some high-powered job with the Minnesota Department of Education, doesn't she?"

"That doesn't mean anything. She thinks she has to be perfect, and she can't—none of us can—so she tries harder and harder. She's going to have a nervous breakdown one of these days." Violet slapped the table for emphasis. "She's one of those who blames herself for her parents' divorce—and her mother's next divorce, and the one after that. And her mother is one of those who let her do it. And now Laurie's making Nellie feel guilty for not being a better daughter."

"How do you know all that?" Penny asked.

"She told me." Aunt Violet smiled complacently. "People like to confide in me."

And have their confidences betrayed. David cleared his throat. "I should get going. I hope Eleanor enjoys the party anyhow."

"She's not going to enjoy it," Brittany snapped. "She's going to be spending the entire evening with her family and a hundred of their friends, all of whom are wondering where she's been and why she's not teaching. She'll have to talk about it and listen to their opinions, all night. She won't have a single person on her side, for support, or just to be a buffer."

David looked at her. She'd worked the entire conversation around to that single statement. She wanted him to know that.

"Why didn't she just say so?" He asked Brittany, ignoring the other two women. Eleanor had said she was desperate for a date, but she hadn't explained. Maybe he hadn't given her a chance.

"She felt guilty," Brittany said. "She liked you, and she knew she'd been wrong to... you know."

David ignored the fascinated stares of Penny and Violet. "Do you think... would it help if I went there? Or would that make it worse?"

"It would be good," she said. "If nothing else, she could use a friend there." She smiled. "A masculine friend. It would be nice if he was well-dressed, handsome, intelligent and charming, especially if he stayed close to her and gave people the impression that she's happy and healthy."

He nodded. "I can see that. Is a tuxedo necessary or will a suit be good enough?"

20

The dress was just a little too short. Not immodest, but about one inch shorter than she'd like. She loved it, otherwise. After four months in blue jeans, Eleanor hardly recognized herself in the midnight blue velvet and lace sheath. Had Laurie remembered how much she liked the style, with a bateau neckline and three-quarter length sleeves, or was it a lucky guess? She tugged at the hem, turning in front of the mirror. At the last minute, she'd pulled the bobby pins from her updo and brushed out her hair. She liked the way the long silver earrings peeked when she moved her head.

The dress was gorgeous, but the shoes... Eleanor tottered over to the bed and picked up her purse. Brittany would appreciate this. She snapped a picture in the mirror and sent it before she could change her mind.

WHAT DO YOU THINK?

The answer was immediate.

NICE! NEW DRESS?

BIRTHDAY GIFT FROM ZACK AND LAURIE. EARRINGS AND SHOES, TOO!

She propped a foot on the bed to take a picture, nearly falling over in the process. Brittany responded before she could send it.

WHEN IS YOUR BIRTHDAY?

Eleanor sent the picture of her shoe and tapped a reply.

NOT TILL APRIL, BUT THEY DECIDED TO GIVE IT
TO ME NOW SO I COULD WEAR IT TO THE PARTY.

She waited a few minutes, but Brittany didn't reply. She didn't have to. They were both thinking the same thing: Laurie wanted to make sure she was dressed appropriately for the party.

"You look beautiful!"

Her mother had said it at least six times, but the mournful note in her voice detracted from the compliment.

"We all look beautiful!" Eleanor gathered Laurie and her mother into a hug. "Thank you for the dress. I love it. And I'll try not to break my neck in these heels. That would ruin the party."

"No ruining the party," Laurie said. "I think we're all ready."

Eleanor surveyed the elegant banquet hall. The musicians were warming up and the caterers, in their black and white uniforms were putting the final touches on the food. "Laurie, this is incredible. The flowers, the tables... and that ice sculpture! I can't believe how perfect it is. You should be an event planner!

Laurie laughed. "I'm pretty happy with my real job." Her pink cheeks and sparkling eyes betrayed her pleasure.

"I think the guests are starting to arrive," Eleanor's dad said, "but it's only six o'clock.

"Oh, no! We aren't ready!" Laurie's voice rose.

Kathy put a hand on her shoulder. "It's perfect. You have it all set up, and now you need to enjoy it. Don't fuss."

"I don't think I know him."

Eleanor turned at her father's voice and looked at the man strolling toward them. She caught her breath.

"Do you know him, Eleanor?" Laurie glanced at her.

"Yes, I do." She hastened toward David, warm with gratitude and pleasure.

He reached out to take her hands, and he smiled.

It was the smile that did it. Eleanor stumbled, staggered, and fell.

She never hit the floor. David scooped her up and cradled her in his arms. "Are you okay?"

His voice was low, and he was asking about more than her ankles. She smiled into his warm, deep, wonderful hazel eyes. "I am now."

"Can you walk?" Her family was nearly upon them, calling anxiously.

"I think so." She slid to her feet. Before she could move away or respond to her parents, he drew her close and kissed the top of her head. He held her like that as the others fell silent.

"Thank you." She breathed the words, hoping he'd understand all of her gratitude. A few seconds later, he released her, leisurely, and turned to meet her family.

He held out his hand. "I'm David Reid, the man your daughter has fallen for."

"This is nice. The fireplace and couches remind me of Uncle Gary's cabin." Eleanor glanced back at the dining room. "And that area's so elegant, all crystal and china. I think I like this better." She dropped onto the couch. "Laurie does know how to throw a party."

David sat next to her, close enough that she could feel his warmth. "The food was amazing."

Eleanor turned to look at him. "I can't even begin to tell you how grateful I am. If you hadn't been here, it would have been one long series of questions and criticism, and not just from my own family." She waved a hand toward the dining room. "All of those people share my parents' priorities. They seem to think we're some kind of scholarly dynasty."

"But you like the work you're doing now, don't you?" David asked.

"I really do. Uncle Gary says he'll pay for me to take a couple classes at the technical college if I'm sure I want to stay."

"Are you sure?" His voice, deep and quiet, gave the question a deeper meaning.

"Yes." Her own voice was a whisper.

He tipped his head toward the party. "Will they be very upset?"

She nodded. No point in denying it. "When I quit teaching, they took it as a personal rejection. And it's not fair. I'm walking on eggshells, trying to make them see I still believe in what they do, but they don't think my work—what I want to do—is as important, and they don't hesitate to say so." She leaned against the cushions. "They've never even asked me about what I do. They're just upset because I'm not doing what they think I should do."

They sat without speaking for a few minutes, gazing at the gas fire. Music and laughter drifted from the dining room, filling the silence.

David stirred. "It's easy to assign relative values to work. People have been doing it forever, even in the church. There's a whole chapter in 1 Corinthians devoted to that problem." He pulled his phone from his jacket pocket and handed it to her. "I've been dealing with some of my own issues there. I made a wallpaper for my lock screen, for when I start second-guessing myself."

Eleanor tapped on the phone and read the words aloud.

"There are different kinds of gifts, but the same Spirit distributes them. There are different kinds of service, but the same Lord. There are different kinds of working, but in all of them and in everyone it is the same God at work."

David took the phone and slid it back into his pocket. "I'm going to finish my seminary classes, but I don't think I'm going to be a regular pastor. I'm not sure what my ministry will look like, and I'm not going to jump into anything until I'm positive."

"What about the rest of it? Do you still want to get married and have children?"

He nodded. "I do. That hasn't changed."

"So..." Eleanor ran a finger across the nap of her

velvet skirt. "Are you going to ask the agency for another match?"

He shifted, bringing their shoulders into contact. "No, I don't think so. That was an awful lot of work. I think I might just keep trying with the match I got."

Eleanor caught her breath. "You didn't get a very good match," she whispered.

"I think I did." He turned her to face him. "I think I got a perfect match. I know it's not what you were looking for, but I think we are a good match. We can be friends, and I think we can be more than friends. I want to try. Will you give me a chance, Eleanor, please?

More than friends. Yes. She pushed back a strand of hair, tangling it in her earring. He worked it free, smoothing the hair behind her ear and moving his hand to cradle the back of her head.

Eleanor gazed up at him, into those beautiful hazel eyes. They held promises of things she'd not dared to hope. A bright future. David saw her for who she was, not who he thought she ought to be. He'd seen the worst in her and still saw the good.

"Yes. Let's try." Eleanor touched his cheek. His skin was warm. "I'd like to try. I'd like that a lot." Her fingers strayed across his lips. "And we are friends already. I think we can start working on the next step."

Happiness flared in Eleanor as he drew her to him. The orchestra embarked on "It's a Wonderful World," and the lyrics filled her heart – and the pounding of her heart drowned out its melody as she anticipated the kiss.

It was tender at first, growing in heat and depth, leaving her breathless, with only one remaining thought: David Reid was her perfect match.

DISCUSSION QUESTIONS

1. In the beginning of this book, Eleanor feels like she can't measure up to the rest of her family, all of whom are successful and confident. It's not a deep, soul-crushing sense of failure but a nagging inferiority complex that prevents her from believing she really fits in. Have you ever felt like that? How did you get past that self-doubt and take your place in your family, church or group of friends? If you are still feeling that way, how are you trying to change the situation?

2. All her life, Eleanor expected to follow in her parents' footsteps, as her brothers did, but now she's realizing it's not what she wants to do. They don't understand, and they put pressure on her. Eleanor knows they care about her and want the best for her. She doesn't want to hurt their feelings or be estranged from them. She values their work and wants to honor them. It can be hard, as a child grows into adulthood and chooses to "disobey" or reject their parents' values and guidance. How can we – as the child or the parent – work through these situations in a way that glorifies God and preserves relationships?

3. Eleanor has run away to "find herself," but David has his life mapped out. He's working as an engineer, going to seminary and intends to become a pastor. He

wants a wife and children, and he wants them now! Those are all good things. Have you ever made plans – all good things – and later realized that you should have been more open to God's direction? How could David – or you – have done that?

4. Eleanor dreaded the prospect of her parents' anniversary party because she knew she'd spend the evening answering questions from a hundred guests. Even though she knew it was really a matchmaking agency, she signed up for Betwixt Two Hearts just to find a date – a presentable man to act as a distraction and buffer, so people wouldn't keep telling her she should come home and go back to teaching. She let her desperation lead her into deceit. How would you have advised or helped her? Can you think of any examples from Scripture in which a person acted rashly because they were afraid?

5. Once she fully understood how wrong it was, she knew she had to tell David the truth. It was hard, not just because she had to confess to her sin, which is always painful, but because she liked him. She knew that when she told him the truth, their budding relationship would be over. He would leave with a poor —but accurate—opinion of her. Our sin has consequences. Have you ever experienced lasting consequences from a sin that was forgiven by God? How do you deal with that situation? Does living with the consequence ever cause you to worry that the sin wasn't really forgiven?

6. David formed a lasting opinion of Angela's

character based on her behavior. Afraid that she was pursuing him, he avoided even public, casual conversation with her. Even when she wanted to come to church (admittedly, to impress and be with him), he only thought of how he could evade her. On the surface, this was a sensible precaution. We think it's wise. But no one in her life was seeing her. Larry listened to her – not even for very long – and realized she needed help. How can we, as ordinary Christian people, watch for people who are hurting, in trouble, or who might need professional help with mental health issues? How do we listen to people like Angela, who look like they might be trouble?

7. David eventually realizes that he may not be called to be a pastor. He still plans to live a life of service and ministry, but he's more open to God's leading, realizing that although his gifts might not be what he thought they were, they are the ones God gave him and still important for God's kingdom.

There are different kinds of gifts, but the same Spirit distributes them. There are different kinds of service, but the same Lord. There are different kinds of working, but in all of them and in everyone it is the same God at work. 1 Corinthians 12:4-6

Sometimes, we value one job or gift over another. This was true in David's mind as well as for Eleanor's family. It can lead to discouragement or pride. How can we respond when we see this happening in our church, family or community?

8. Violet Anderson values family history as well as living relationships. It grieves her that the younger generations only look forward and aren't interested in their ancestors. She's never married or had children of her own, but she tries to hold the extended family together. They are all getting married (gaining in-laws) and having babies, too busy to make the extended family a priority. What do you think? Is the extended family a dying institution? Looking at Scripture, what instances can you find of this?

9. Many families have an Uncle Olof. Do you? Alzheimer's and dementia are common problems, painful for the victim and their loved ones. Eleanor is uncomfortable with lying to Uncle Olof instead of encouraging him to remember people. She finds it "creepy" that little Sarah doesn't mind him thinking she's his sister and calling her Violet while they play checkers. What do you think? Do you have a loved one with dementia or Alzheimer's? How would you engage with a person in Uncle Olof's condition?

About the Author

After 40 years of wandering (but always in lovely places and not in a desert), Cathe Swanson has recently returned to her childhood home and family in Minnesota.

In the summer, she and her husband enjoy spending time with their grandchildren and being outdoors, gardening, hiking, birdwatching, and kayaking. The long winters are perfect for playing games, reading, and indoor hobbies. Cathe's been a quilter and teacher of quiltmaking for nearly 30 years and enjoys just about any kind of creative work, especially those involving fiber or paper.

Everything inspires new books! Cathe's Swedish heritage, love of quilting, and an interest in genealogy led to The Glory Quilts series. The Hope Again series is inspired by her life in the Midwest and experiences with the elderly, the military, and inner-city ministry. As a child of the 60's, she's having fun writing about hippies and the Jesus People movement in the Serenity Hill series.

More Books by Cathe Swanson

The Hope Again Series

Baggage Claim
Snow Angels
Long Shadows
Hope for the Holidays
Home Run
Christmas at the Unity Plenkiss

The Glory Quilts Series

Always and Forever
Matched Hearts

The Serenity Hill Series

Season of Change
Starting Now (Spring 2022)

Potato Flake Christmas
Murder at the Empire

Made in the USA
Coppell, TX
13 September 2021

62317875R00125